My Forever Plus-One

DARING DIVORCEES

BOOK THREE

SHANNYN SCHROEDER

Cover created by Kari March Designs

This title was originally published by Entangled in 2019.

ISBN: 978-1-950640-59-1

Newsletter

If you'd like to stay up-to-date on my releases and have the chance to win some prizes, join my newsletter on my website - www.ShannynSchroeder.com

And you can check out my other series:

The O'Leary Family

The O'Malley Family

The Doyle Family

Hot & Nerdy

Daring Divorcees

Counterfeit Capers (writing as Sloane Steele)

Chapter One

Evelyn Rhodes tossed the headset onto the console just as the director yelled, "Cut." Another day, another group of young women armed with the knowledge of which men had fathered their children. As she turned to leave the control room, the new intern, Aisha, came barreling through the door.

"Mr. Edmundson wants you to come to his office."

Evelyn looked through the glass to the stage where everyone was shutting down.

Aisha leaned closer and lowered her voice. "I think he means right now."

Evelyn nodded. Harry always wanted everything right now. She scanned her memory for a reason he would demand her presence. Not sweeps week. No fights had broken out on-camera recently, so there was no legal action.

"I'm coming," she said as a means to dismiss Aisha. Before heading upstairs, she stopped by her office for a fresh cup of coffee, even though it was a mistake to drink more at four in the afternoon.

She shook her hair loose from the ponytail she swept it up in for the duration of filming. Then she slipped her blazer back on. Although she and Harry were friendly enough to be on a first-name basis, he was still her boss. She always appeared professional in front of him.

Outside Harry's office on the eighth floor, his secretary waved her in. Evelyn edged through the door and asked, "Leave it open?"

Whether the door remained open or closed often hinted at the topic of the meeting. Harry always liked the door closed if he was going to yell. Not that the solid wood kept the conversation muffled. Harry had a booming voice that carried everywhere.

"Closed."

Damn. She gave the door a gentle push and crossed the room. Harry pointed to the chairs in front of his desk without looking up. As she stared at the top of his scalp peeking through snowy white hair, she pondered what might've happened that she could be held responsible for. She came up with nothing.

She sipped her coffee and waited. Harry had a great corner office that overlooked the lower half of the Loop. The TV station wasn't one of the major networks, but as far as a local station went, they did pretty well. She often considered if she would like his job—in this office—but she wasn't ready to give up her time in the trenches. She liked to be hands-on.

"How are things downstairs?" He made eye contact,

a soft smile on his face. He leaned back in his chair and rolled his shirtsleeves to his elbows.

"Good." She cradled her cup and tried to decipher where he was going.

"I have some news. Well, more like rumors."

"Whatever it is, I didn't do it," she said with a smirk. "Unless it's good. Then I'll take credit."

That drew a laugh from him. "The Women in Media group will announce the nominees for their annual awards soon."

This wasn't news to her. Early on in her career, she'd waited for them eagerly, sure she would at least get nominated. More than a decade later, she no longer held out hope.

Harry leaned forward, pressing his forearms on his desk. "I think this is your year."

"What?"

"Nothing official yet, but I have friends who think you're getting nominated."

She smiled and gripped her cup tighter to prevent herself from jumping up and dancing.

"Needless to say, having an award-winning producer on staff would be a boon for the station."

And it would finally be her chance to pitch the show she'd been thinking about for months, holding out for just the right time. She'd thought sweeps week would be good —at least if they performed well. But this…this was better.

"Don't go telling anyone yet, but I wanted to give you the heads-up."

"Thank you." As long as his intel was good, and really, Harry wouldn't say anything unless he was sure.

"While I'm here, if you have a few more minutes, I have something I'd like to run by you."

"Shoot."

"I've been thinking about developing a new show. Trent Talks is doing well, and Luke or Tanya could take over producing."

Harry sat back in his oversize leather chair, propped his elbows on the armrests, and steepled his fingers. At least she had his attention.

"I'd like to do a morning talk show. Something lighter, like feel-good Oprah. I have an acquaintance who would be fabulous. She's not a journalist, but she's the kind of person that others open up to."

"There are already a crap-ton of morning talk shows. How would you stand out?"

"I want it to be Chicago-centric. We have a wealth of brilliant people right here in our city who are fascinating. I'm not saying we would never have outside guests, like celebrities visiting the city for performances and such, but I want to primarily focus on locals. Authors, CEOs, actors, musicians. Give our people a shout-out on TV. Show the world that Chicago is more than rats, guns, and pizza."

He nodded, his fingers rubbing against his lips, but he said nothing. Evelyn wasn't giving him a full-blown pitch, but with Harry, it was good to strike whenever given the chance.

"I'll think about it. Get me some numbers, staffing, and show ideas and we'll talk again."

"I'll have it to you by next week." She rose. "Thanks for your time."

"Keep doing what you're doing. You're one of our best."

With another smile and nod, she headed out of his office. She contained her excitement until she got to the elevator. On her way down, she shimmied a little dance and texted Owen to tell him to come over for dinner.

OWEN HANSON TOOK OFF HIS HELMET AND SET IT ON THE head of a seven-year-old who looked up at him in awe. His phone buzzed in his pocket, but pulling it out from under his turnout gear was a pain in the ass, so whoever was texting would have to wait.

"Hey, Owen. Can you take a picture of us by the truck?" Sam called as he ran by.

Owen looked down at little Hector, whose head was swallowed by the helmet. He tilted the brim so he could see the boy's face. "Hold on to that for me, would you?"

Hector smiled and nodded, knocking the brim back down over his eyes.

Owen turned back to the fire truck, where a group of teenage boys were huddled near the door. They were tough kids who would never admit to wanting to hang around the truck, but his firehouse stopped by the youth center a couple of times a year, and they always had a crowd. He took a couple shots with Sam's phone, one with the boys smiling and one with them all making faces.

Sam raced back for his phone. "Thanks."

Sandra, the center's director, came up beside him. "They love this, you know."

"Yeah. Fire trucks bring out the kid in all of us."

She shook her head. "It's more than that. Even though you've told them that you're a firefighter, it doesn't really click until they see this." She pointed at the truck and then at him in his gear. "This shows them that a real hero spends time with them. Cares about them."

His cheeks warmed. He loved his job, but this kind of comment made him uneasy. "I'm not a hero. I just do my job."

"Don't sell yourself short. These kids don't interact with enough positive role models. For weeks after this, they'll be looking at you with stars in their eyes."

He did these visits as a way to talk about fire safety and give the older kids a chance to see that they had options for real careers. It was never about painting himself as a hero. But he thought back to his childhood and the field trip to the firehouse that had made him decide his career path. He'd looked at those firefighters as heroes, too. Now he worked with a lot of good men, none of whom considered themselves heroes.

An hour later, he was riding in the jump seat to return to the station. He wasn't on duty today, so all he had to do was turn in his gear. On the short trip back to the house, he finally pulled out his phone. The text he'd missed was from Evelyn telling him to come over for dinner.

"Hey, I know that look. Someone just got a sext from a hottie," Jamal said beside him.

Owen shook his head. He dismissed most of what

came out of Jamal's mouth because the guy was young. "I'm too old for that shit."

"Never too old for naked women."

"I don't need a picture. I like the live-and-in-person version." He tucked his phone away. "And that was just Evelyn."

Jamal groaned. "It's always just Evelyn. Man, if you ain't gonna hit that, she should be open market."

Owen shot him another look. "Evelyn is off-limits."

"Why? Afraid of a little competition?"

"There is no competition."

"So you don't want her, but no one else can have her?"

"Yeah, something like that." It wasn't about wanting or not wanting her. He couldn't have her. Or at least he shouldn't. But the thought of Evelyn being with a guy he worked with rubbed him wrong. She dated other people, just like he did. But she held a special place in his life. The one person he could count on, no matter what. "I highly doubt you could handle a woman like her anyway."

Jamal barked out laughter and began listing his various sexual conquests. Owen let him ramble because he knew Jamal didn't have a chance. It was one of the unwritten rules he had with Evelyn. They didn't date each other's colleagues because it would mess with their friendship.

While Jamal talked, Owen pulled his phone back out and asked Evelyn if he should pick up dinner.

Got it covered.

8?

Better make it 8:30 otherwise I'll be late.

Like every day.

She sent back a middle finger emoji. Her favorite symbol. But she knew he was right. She always said she was going to be home earlier than she was. It was one of the reasons he had a key to her condo. At least a few nights a week, they had dinner together and hung out. He'd gotten tired of sitting in his car waiting on her, so she'd given him a key. Doing that had saved their friendship.

Before he had a chance to put his phone away, Tara texted to see if he was free for dinner. He paused. They'd gone on a couple dates, and he enjoyed her company, but there was nothing special there. Was she worth skipping dinner with Evelyn?

Weighing what his night might look like, he responded that he already had plans.

They pulled into the station, and the guys all hopped out and stowed their gear. After saying goodbye to everyone and thanking the captain for letting him borrow the truck for the youth center, he drove straight to Evelyn's house. Even though she wouldn't be home for a couple hours, he'd find something to watch on TV while he waited.

THAT NIGHT, EVELYN WAS STILL RIDING THE HIGH OF A possible award nomination. It was silly, especially because the information was based on gossip, but she wanted it. She'd tried to convince herself that awards and recognition like that didn't matter, but part of her wanted others to know how good she was. She wasn't just some cute girl who'd slept her way into her position. She'd earned her way there, and the award would prove it.

Owen's car was already parked in the guest spot for her condo, which was no surprise. He routinely made himself at home in her place. She did the same at his.

Honestly, she preferred his place. He had a small house with a cute yard for his dog, Probie. She loved being greeted by Probie. The huge dog acted like a poodle, always trying to climb on her lap for love. Her condo was nice, but not homey. Even though she'd lived there for the better part of a decade, it was still just a place to live. She'd grown up in a house where something was always falling apart and her mother had never had the time or money to fix it. She'd promised herself that she wouldn't live like that when she was grown.

Of course, it took until she was grown to understand what home ownership meant. She'd never wanted a house because of the upkeep. Like her single mom, she worked too many hours to devote to things like maintenance, which was why she enjoyed Owen's place. He took care of everything.

She smiled as she rode the elevator up to her floor. Hell, he took care of everything in her place, too. She never called the building maintenance guy. Owen just fixed things. She sometimes wondered why her mom hadn't had an Owen in her life. There had been boyfriends here and there, but no one reliable. Evelyn couldn't even remember any of their names.

As she unlocked the door, she heard the murmur of the TV. Setting her keys on the counter, she listened. Damn. It didn't sound like sports, which meant Owen was watching a movie. He only watched two kinds of movies—action and old black-and-white ones. She could handle a cheesy action flick, but the old movies always put her to sleep.

She walked to the living room and found Owen asleep on her couch. Sure enough, on the TV was a movie made in the forties. She nudged him with her leg as she sidled past to put the food on the table. "Wake up, Grandpa."

He stretched, his blue Chicago Fire Department T-shirt riding up. She shouldn't want to peek at that, but what sane woman could resist? The trail of hair that led into his pants was sexy.

Damn Nina for making her rethink her life. Last summer, when their friend Tess was debating stepping back into the dating pool, Nina had challenged everyone in their support group to actively look for partners for their lives. They had all been divorced for years, and they had come together as friends based on the idea of moving on with their lives after divorce. In their New Beginnings group, both Tess and Trevor had found love after Nina's prodding.

Evelyn, not so much.

She also hadn't found herself checking out her best friend until Nina had pointed out that she and Owen should be more than friends.

His biceps flexed as he rubbed his hands over his face. "Huh?"

"Between the old movie and you falling asleep before the sun sets, you're like a grandpa." Shoving thoughts of Nina and her silly challenge aside, she plopped next to him.

He pinched her thigh playfully. "I had a long day. Took the truck to the youth center for the kids."

"Sounds like an excuse to me. I've been up since five thirty."

"Whatever. What'd you get for dinner?" He slid forward and began ripping open bags. "Burgers," he said almost reverently.

He loved a good burger.

"You spoil me."

"This is an almost-celebration dinner."

"A what?"

She accepted the Styrofoam container he handed her. "Harry called me into his office today. It's not official yet, but he thinks I'm up for an award from Women in Media."

He squinted at her as he chewed his food. "Is that the one you drag me to every year? I have to wear a tux and fake smile and politely clap the whole time you're miserable?"

She'd just taken a bite of burger and choked at his

description. She shouldn't laugh, but he was basically right. While she continued to cough into her napkin, Owen got up and got them drinks. After a few sips, she was able to breathe. She wiped her eyes. "It doesn't make me miserable to be there. I know some of the people nominated. It's a networking thing. See people and be seen."

"Sure," he said completely unconvincingly. "What about all the fake smiling?"

"The whole business is fake." He hated that part of her job. She wasn't too fond of it, either, but she did what was necessary. She ate some more of her food.

"If this is your celebration, why are we eating my favorite food?"

"Food isn't as important to me as it is to you. If I win, I'll celebrate with champagne. This is big."

He set his burger down. Looking straight into her eyes, he said, "I'm not trying to say that it's not. I'm proud of you. They'd be stupid to not recognize how good you are at your job."

He had no idea whether or not she was any good at her job, but his pride was genuine. It was one of the many reasons he was the first person she turned to with good news. He supported her even when he didn't fully understand. That kind of unconditional love was hard to come by. "And if I win, I'll have the clout I need to push for creating the new show I've been thinking about."

"Finally tired of 'Who's the Baby Daddy' episodes?"

"I want to do a daytime talk with a local spin."

He nodded but asked, "What does that mean?"

"It means I'll have a host—you remember Marilyn? I

introduced you at a charity thing last summer—anyway, we've talked on occasion. She'd be perfect for the camera, and she has connections all over the city. She can reach anyone."

"Anyone?"

"If she doesn't have the connection, she knows someone who does. People like her. She can get them to talk and keep it interesting. I've never seen someone work a room like she does. Plus, she's gorgeous. The audience will eat it up."

He finished the last of his burger and sipped from the can of pop. "Why don't you do it?"

She gave him a look like he'd lost his mind. "I'm not a host. I hate being in front of the camera."

"Why? You're as gorgeous as Marilyn. And people talk to you all the time."

"I'm not an on-camera personality. I couldn't do it. Besides, I'd get fired after I dropped a few F-bombs. That's a huge no-no on camera." She ate a few more bites of her burger before handing him the rest.

Of course, he wolfed it down. She couldn't even be jealous that he ate like that. He worked out all the time to stay in shape for his job. She, on the other hand, only grudgingly walked on the treadmill a few times a week. She'd rather eat only half the burger and not have to work out.

Owen scooped up all of their trash and took it to the kitchen. Evelyn slipped off her shoes and changed the channel before he came back.

"What did Harry say?"

"About what?" she asked absently as she caught the start of the local news. Heatwave at the tail end of summer in the city. Another shoot-out in a Chicago neighborhood. A bystander killed.

Owen muted the TV. "What did Harry say about your show idea? You told him about it, didn't you?"

She blinked and turned her focus to him. "Kind of. I knew I had to strike while he was having good thoughts about me. So I mentioned it, but I didn't give him a formal pitch. He told me to run some numbers and he'd take a look."

Owen snorted.

"What?"

"If you've been thinking about it, you already have a pitch and numbers and everything Harry could possibly want. It's what you do."

Her skin warmed. Sometimes she forgot how well he knew her. He acted like he didn't pay attention to things, but he did. "Well, it's not like I carry the information around with me."

He shot her a look. "But you have it."

"Yes. But that's not the way things work. Especially with Harry. He needs to be eased into it. If I just whipped out a file to give him the full plan, he'd feel blindsided."

"Instead, you're going to weasel your way in?"

"Not quite the way I would put it, but yeah." She settled back into the couch, leaning against him comfortably. "Weaseling. Schmoozing. It's the glamorous life I lead."

"I'll take the danger of a fire over schmoozing any day." His arm settled around her shoulder. "Mike and Abby are having their end-of-the-season cookout Sunday. You coming?"

"Sure. What should I bring?"

"Something store-bought."

"I'm not that bad a cook," she said, giving him a shove.

"Sure." He paused and then said, "Watch out for Jamal."

"Why?" She thought about the young firefighter who was always quick with a joke or a boastful story.

"He thinks he has a shot to be with you."

"Oh, really? And why wouldn't he?"

He stiffened against her. "Would you want to go out with him?"

Sometimes Owen made it far too easy to fuck with him. "We both know he's not looking to date me. He is a young, good-looking guy. I bet his stamina is amazing."

Owen grunted.

"Down, boy. I'm teasing." She stifled a laugh. She was far past the point of playing with boys. She was old enough to understand the value of a good man. "How did the youth center go today?"

"Good. The usual. Kids love the truck. Little ones like to play with our gear."

"Everything you do for that center and the kids…it's cool. You're a good guy."

"Not so good that I'm letting you get away with changing the channel." He snatched the remote and put his movie back on. "Trust me. You'll like this one."

She didn't care about the movie but she couldn't complain about hanging with her best friend, while stretched out on her couch, watching something he enjoyed. Today had been a good day.

OWEN USED HIS KEY TO LET HIMSELF INTO EVELYN'S condo. He didn't bother ringing first, because he knew she wouldn't be ready, and making her stop to answer the door would just make them later. When she was his date for an event, he always gave her the wrong time, because she was always late.

But since they were going to Tess's engagement party, and Tess was a friend to both of them, he couldn't lie about what time to be ready.

"I'm here," he called out.

She peeked around the corner that led to her bedroom. "Almost ready," she said with a wink.

If the shimmery blue strap on her shoulder was any indication, she wasn't even dressed. He sighed. "Got any beer?"

"In the fridge. But you know there's an open bar, right?"

"Yeah, but Miles's family is throwing this party, and there's no telling what hoity-toity shit they'll have." He liked Tess's boyfriend—fiancé. He was a good guy who treated Tess and her kids well. But he came from money. The kind of money guys like Owen never even considered a possibility in this lifetime.

"They're rich. That means top-shelf liquor all the way," she yelled.

Maybe she had a point. He looked in her fridge and saw she only had two bottles. They were his favorite beer, which she kept just for him. He couldn't remember the last time she had something in the fridge for anyone else.

He grabbed a glass and filled it with water. Leaning against the kitchen counter, he scrolled through his phone.

"Wow. Talk about a GQ moment," she said.

He looked up from his phone, and like a cartoon character, his tongue almost rolled out of his mouth to drag on the floor.

Their gazes locked and something passed between them. A charged, heated look that told him she sometimes had the same passionate thoughts about them that he had. Then she blinked. *Did I imagine the silent conversation?*

"New suit?" she asked while fiddling with earrings. Her head tilted to shift her hair out of her way, exposing her long neck.

He nodded, unsure of his ability to form words. He thought he'd seen Evelyn in every kind of dress and suit imaginable. But this dress made her mouth-wateringly beautiful. It was the same shimmery blue of whatever she had on underneath—he had to work to prevent himself from thinking about that—and it hugged every part of her.

"Wow," he finally blurted.

She smiled and curtsied. "Thank you. That's the reaction I was going for."

His heart rate kicked up. She wanted him to have that reaction? He swallowed hard. "You're even more stunning than usual."

She stepped closer and patted his chest. "You're

looking pretty good yourself. What made you break down and finally get a new suit?"

"I got tired of you telling me I was being cheap by not buying one."

"I don't think I ever called you cheap. But you did wear that suit for a decade."

"It fit."

She sighed in a way that said he was hopeless.

"Ready to go?"

"Yep." She held up her purse and turned to leave.

His eyes trailed from the sexy heels that made her nearly his height, up over bare legs to the curve of her ass. That's when he saw that the back of her dress didn't exist. An expanse of bare skin for anyone to see. He continued to talk to distract himself. "I still can't believe Tess asked Miles to marry her."

Evelyn looked over her shoulder. "Why?"

"Didn't it bother Miles?"

She turned completely around. "Is this some macho guy thing? It's the man's job to propose?"

Heat crawled up his neck. Evelyn had a habit of calling him out for being a Neanderthal. He didn't think he was acting like a caveman; he was just old-fashioned. "I'm traditional."

She tilted her head and studied him. "Even now, after everything with Stacy? You already did the whole down-on-one-knee, big wedding thing."

"What does she have to do with anything?"

"I've never heard you talk about marriage. Hell, I never thought you'd trust another woman enough to want to tie yourself to her."

He shrugged. "I didn't say I was looking to get

married again, just that if I did, I would want to pop the question."

He considered admitting that she was the only woman he'd trusted in a long time, but then again, they were friends. They weren't sleeping together, so she couldn't cheat on him. But marriage? Could he open himself up for that again?

They walked out to the hallway, and Evelyn locked up. Another thought occurred to him because of her questioning.

"You think you'll remarry?" he asked. It wasn't something that he'd really considered with them. Even as their friends were falling in love and starting new lives, he thought he and Evelyn would always have each other. But if she got married…

"I don't know. I'm not actively looking, if that's what you're wondering." She pressed the elevator button. "But there's part of me that misses having someone to come home to."

The elevator doors swooshed open. She took his arm and leaned close. "And regular sex. I miss regular sex," she said in a low voice.

He jabbed the button for the lobby. Evelyn talking about sex shouldn't have his dick perking up. He knew that, but his dick obviously didn't. He cleared his throat. "I'm pretty sure you could get laid whenever you want."

She laid her head on his shoulder with a sigh. "A random hookup isn't the same."

Her body pressed against him made him think about getting laid. Her soft curves lined up along his body, and he briefly imagined her lying beneath him.

Of course she was right. She wasn't talking about

getting off. That was easy to find, but the connection with someone who mattered was something they both missed. They had that connection with each other, albeit not quite the same.

On the way to the party, Evelyn chatted about work. Then they talked about his brother's wedding, which was coming up in a little over a month.

"Did you schedule your vacation days?" he asked.

"Yes. Did you?"

"I put in the request the minute my brother gave me dates. You never need to check up on me."

"Yeah, yeah...you always have your shit together."

He pulled into the hotel's circular drive to the valet stand.

"Ooo...I feel special. You're using the valet instead of making me hike from a parking garage."

He pointed at the heels she wore. "I doubt you could hike anywhere in those."

The valet opened her door, and she stepped out. After he accepted the ticket and joined her, she turned a leg out, flashing more skin than he wanted anyone to see.

"Don't you like them?"

"They look phenomenal, and they do amazing things for your legs, but they're not made for hiking. And I'm not about to carry you." He made the joke to prevent himself from thinking about exactly how good her legs looked and what the heels did for her ass. He checked the urge to reach out and grab a handful. Over the years he'd learned restraint.

She took his arm again. "Whatever happened to chivalry?"

"It died with the invention of the internet and Tinder."

"And dick pics," she added with a laugh. She patted his biceps. "There are a few chivalrous guys left, though."

He led her through the lobby and to the elevators. Tess and Miles had chosen to have the party at the rooftop restaurant of the hotel where they'd first met, which was also where Tess had proposed. Owen felt out of place surrounded by so many people with huge bank accounts. They wore suits that cost as much as one of his paychecks. The jewelry hanging on the women sparkled enough to blind him.

But for his friends, he'd suck it up and try to have a good time. As a waiter walked by with a tray of champagne glasses, he snagged one for Evelyn and handed it to her. "I'll be back in a minute. I'm going to see what's available at the bar."

"Stay out of trouble. I'll find Nina and Trevor."

Chapter Two

Evelyn sipped her champagne as she watched Owen walk toward the bar. Something was different about him tonight—other than the new suit. If she didn't know better, she'd think a woman had dressed him. The suit fit his body perfectly. Although he would never spend money on custom-made, he'd done well with that purchase.

One of the things she loved about Owen was his view on money. He liked to be comfortable but wouldn't spend frivolously. In his mind, he saw no reason to spend an extra three hundred on a suit when that same three hundred could buy new equipment for the youth center. Regardless of what he said, he was a good guy—chivalrous to the core.

Turning away, she went to find their friends from the New Beginnings group. No dinner tonight, only appetizers and drinks, but the appetizers looked downright amazing. She could make a meal of them. She took a stuffed mushroom off a tray and popped it in her mouth. She surveyed the area, taking in the guests. Tess had a small family, but it looked like Miles's mother had invited every who's who in the city.

She found Nina, Trevor, and Callie at a high-top table. It was a four-seater, but they could drag a chair over for Owen. "Hey," she said, setting her glass on the table. She walked around and gave Nina and Trevor hugs. She waved at Callie. Although she liked Trevor's girlfriend, they weren't hug-level friends. At least not yet. "No Gabe tonight?"

Trevor said, "He's on his way."

Evelyn looked to the bar to keep an eye out for Owen. When she caught his eye, she waved.

"Did you come with someone?" Callie asked.

She nodded. "Owen."

"Owen? Like Owen, Owen?"

Nina leaned on the table as Owen joined them. "Of course our Owen. As always."

"Not—" Evelyn started to argue, but then she realized that Nina was right. They were always each other's plus-one. They never considered coming with anyone else. At least she never thought about it. *Does Owen?*

"Our Owen, what?" he asked, setting a glass of beer next to her arm.

"Callie asked who my date was."

"But you're not..." Callie pointed back and forth between them.

"No," they answered simultaneously.

They must've spoken too loudly or something, because Callie dropped it. Nina, however, gave them both the stink eye. Ever since issuing her challenge, Nina had been hounding Evelyn and Owen. She had told them to shit or get off the pot. As if something was supposed to happen between them. But that look they'd shared earlier in her kitchen had her thinking...

Owen must've noticed Nina's meddling glare, too, because he said, "Want to dance?"

"Sure." Evelyn took his hand, and he led her to the dance floor.

A slow song was playing, which was probably the only reason he'd asked. He didn't normally dance.

He put an arm around her waist, his palm was warm against the bare skin of her back. His other hand held hers. As they began to sway, she tried to ignore the caress of his fingers, so she asked, "Do you ever think about bringing someone else as your plus one?"

"Nope."

"Why not?"

"Who else would I have a better time with besides my best friend?"

She brought her chin close to his shoulder. Their bodies brushed with each shift. "I don't know. Maybe someone you'll get lucky with?"

He chuckled, and she felt the vibrations through her entire body. That kind of laugh coming from any other guy would have her thinking about getting naked. It was bad enough that it sent a tingle through her.

"Hey, I'm open to all possibilities." His low voice caused another rush of warmth.

His comment caused a hitch in her step. She had no idea if he was still joking. For the next verse of the song, she stayed silent and remembered how good it had been the one time they'd thrown all reason aside and slept with each other. They had met in the divorce support group almost a year before Trevor, Tess, and Gabe joined. Nina had come along even later.

That early on, she and Owen had been raw and hurting, but the chemistry had been there.

They'd gone out for drinks after a meeting and had ended up at her place. It had been the first time for both of them post-divorce. As much as it had simply been a stepping stone toward healing, it had been one of the hottest nights of her life.

She had come from a divorce feeling undesirable and worthless. She couldn't do something as basic as keep a man. Worse, as soon as the ink dried on the papers, her ex had found someone new. Evelyn had still been reeling from the collapse of a relationship she'd believed would last forever.

That night, Owen had managed to be rough yet tender as he'd explored her body. They'd fucked all night—from being buzzed straight through sobriety, as if chasing out the bad memories that divorce had created.

Finally, she swallowed. "I thought we agreed that wasn't a smart move."

The song ended, but they continued to move. "That was before—"

His response was cut off by Miles calling for attention at the front of the room. Owen stepped back but didn't let go of her hand. Her heart raced. She wanted to yank him away from the crowd and ask what he was about to say, but Miles was toasting Tess.

While they listened to speeches about the happy couple, Evelyn considered the possibilities of what Owen hadn't said. Ultimately, she decided not to ask him. They'd been right all those years ago. They'd helped each other heal. Owen had been her best friend, her rock, ever since. Whenever she doubted herself, he was there to shore her up. When he believed there was something fundamentally wrong with him, she pointed out how great he was. Changing their relationship would mean changing his role in her life, and she couldn't imagine losing that.

What they had was special. No way was she willing to risk it for some phenomenal sex.

EVELYN HAD JUST STEPPED OUT OF THE SHOWER AND WAS rushing through her room to find something to wear when her phone rang.

"I'll be there in thirty."

Shit *Shit!* "I'll meet you there."

Owen's sigh was heavy. "How long?"

"What do you mean?"

"How long until you're ready?"

"Not sure. Just go ahead. I'll be right behind you."

"I can come and wait for you."

Owen detested being late. She didn't want to ruin his afternoon by making him late. He'd never say it, but he'd be a total grump. She knew better than to try to convince him that arriving at any time other than when the party started was no big deal.

"You hate waiting for me."

"Yet I do it all the time."

"I'll meet you at Mike and Abby's. I'll be there soon." She shimmied into her shorts with her phone in the crook of her neck. "I'm getting dressed now. I already have the dessert I'm bringing."

Another sigh. She could almost hear the thoughts being weighed back and forth—show up late with her or on time alone.

"Last time you were on your own to meet me, you almost missed the whole thing."

"That was different." She'd been caught up at work and lost track of time. She chuckled and rolled her eyes. "Go. I'll see you soon."

He didn't respond.

"I promise," she said.

"Okay. See you there."

She tossed her phone on the bed and finished getting ready. Knowing Owen would drive her home, she took a ride-share. She tipped the driver and scooped up the two trays of desserts (store-bought) she was bringing as her contribution to the potluck meal.

A bright yellow sign hung on the front door telling guests to come around back. She loved coming to parties like this with Owen. His circle of friends accepted her without thought of what she could do for them. Throughout her marriage to Donald, every event had been a networking opportunity. People wanted to get close to her because she could take them to Donald, and her husband never entered into a relationship unless he could get something from it. But with Owen, she never had to perform. She was free to be herself.

Around here, she was simply Owen's friend. She reached over the gate to flip the lever. As soon as the gate swung open, the full force of party noises hit her. Music blared from speakers near the patio door. A small kiddie pool in the corner of the yard held a few young children who were squealing and splashing.

She rounded the corner of the house to look for Owen. She was comforted by all of the familiar faces she saw. Some people offered a smile and nod of acknowledgment, others a wave. Then there was Abby, who rushed at her and squeezed her in a tight hug.

"It's about time you got here."

"I'm not that late."

"No, but Owen has been staring at the gate waiting for you, like a puppy waiting for someone to come home."

Evelyn rolled her eyes. Owen was not dying to see her. Abby had a flair for the dramatic. "Here." She thrust the desserts at the woman.

Abby took the trays and threaded her other arm through Evelyn's. "You're not getting away that easily. I haven't seen you in forever. Why don't you come around more often?"

"I show up whenever Owen tells me there's a party."

"You don't need Owen's invitation. You can join us whenever you want. We have book club once a month."

"I don't have that much spare time for reading."

Abby laughed. "We call it book club. We buy the book and sometimes we might read part of it. Mostly, we sit around, drink wine, and gossip."

The drinking wine part sounded good. And really, she should put in the effort to make more friends. She had Tess and Nina, but other than that, she didn't have many female friends. Most of the people she worked with were men, except for some of the interns. Her world lacked connections with women.

"Who's in the book club?" Abby led her to a long table already weighed down with food. "Other firefighter wives."

And there was the rub. "I'm not a firefighter wife."

Abby set the desserts down and turned to face her. "First, there are no requirements for joining. Second, you're the closest thing Owen has ever had to a wife. I mean, since his divorce, anyway. Does the man even date? He's never brought anyone around except you."

"Well, we do tend to be each other's plus-one wherever we go." *We're safe for each other. No worries about friends forming attachments with people who might not stick around.*

"Think about it. I'll get your email from Owen and send you info."

"Sounds good." But Evelyn doubted she would join. Too many assumptions would be made if she showed up. As much as she loved Owen, she wasn't part of his work family.

Abby yelled across the yard at one of the kids, so Evelyn took that as her cue to grab something to eat while she was standing there. Considering Abby had told her Owen had been waiting for her, it was odd that she still didn't see him. She picked up a brownie that looked deliciously homemade and took a bite.

Oh, yeah, homemade.

She glanced around the yard again and her eyes landed on Owen. He was with a couple of guys she didn't know well. He smiled at her and lifted his arm as if to look at an imaginary watch. She winked and took another bite of brownie. She turned to grab a napkin and came face-to-face with Jamal.

"Hey, Evelyn. Long time no see." He leaned in and gave her a hug.

"How are you, Jamal?"

"Good. I told Owen he should invite you out more often."

What was with these people? It seemed like with every event, more of them made similar comments. "I see Owen all the time."

"But he doesn't bring you around us."

"Well, if it's a firefighter thing, I don't really belong."

"Come on, now. You're one of us." He put an arm around her shoulder and turned her back to face the yard. "Look around. Everyone knows you."

For the first time, she really paid attention. She did know these people. And they knew her. Was it enough for them to know her? Did that make her fit in? Belong?

"Hey, didn't I tell you Evelyn was off-limits?" Owen said from her other side.

"We're all innocent here," Jamal said with a smirk. "Unless Evelyn doesn't want to stay innocent."

She barked out a laugh. "My innocence left the building a long time ago."

Jamal dropped his arm. "Who's up for a game of cornhole?"

"Maybe a little later," she said. As Jamal walked away, she nudged Owen. "That wasn't nice. He wasn't hitting on me."

Owen raised an eyebrow.

"Okay, at the end there, he was. But that was just for your benefit. Before that, he was being friendly."

"Uh-huh."

"What do you care, anyway?"

"It would complicate my life, and I prefer things simple."

She didn't have a comeback for that. It would complicate his life. But she wasn't attracted to Jamal. She was over young guys.

"What were you guys looking at, anyway?"

"Jamal was pointing out that I belong here, I guess. And for the first time, I realized that coming here is kind of like hanging out with family. Without the stress."

One of the many things that drew her to Owen was his sense of family. He had his own family and his work family, and he had quickly brought her into all of it. It had been him who suggested coffee after the divorce support group. He made friends with Trevor and then Tess and so on. The group had grown because of him. She'd simply enjoyed the result.

"You are family." He said it matter-of-factly. As if there were no question.

"The other guys bring wives and girlfriends. I'm neither."

"You're better. You're my best friend. Now let's go show Jamal how the game is played." He took her hand and led her across the yard.

Monday morning, Owen walked into Sunny's Diner to meet his friends. Trevor and Tess sat at the table, already drinking coffee. Owen nodded at the waitress as he made his way over.

"Hey," he said as he sat.

Trevor looked over. "I have some stuff for you. For the center. Evan's clearing out the storage shed. There's lumber and leftover materials if you want it. I figured you could do some kind of project with the kids."

"Cool. I'll swing by after my next shift and pick it up."

Tess leaned forward as the waitress filled his cup. He turned over the one next to his because he saw Nina crossing the parking lot.

"Where's Evelyn?"

"She had to go in to work early. Today's the day they announce the nominations for the Women in Media Awards. Her boss thinks she's getting nominated this year."

Tess's eyes widened. "Really? That's awesome. When will she know?"

He shrugged. Although Evelyn had called him this morning and chatted nervously on her way to work, she hadn't said when the call was happening.

"When will who know what?" Nina asked as she took a seat across from him.

Tess said, "Evelyn is up for some TV award. She finds out if she's been nominated today."

"Why didn't she say anything?"

"She told Owen," Tess pointed out.

Nina rolled her eyes. "She tells Owen everything. Why didn't she tell us?"

"I don't know." He drank from his cup. "Maybe because every year she hopes to be nominated, and it doesn't happen. It would drive her crazy to have everyone feel sorry for her."

"Makes sense," Trevor said.

They fell into a brief silence until Nina spoke again. "The party was awesome, Tess. I couldn't have organized it better myself."

"Thanks. I would've had you do it, but Miles's mom has her own people. That family has people for everything. It's a little overwhelming."

Trevor chuckled. "Since the engagement party was so over-the-top, what are you going to do for the wedding?"

Tess shrugged.

"Speaking of weddings," Nina interjected, "what's happening with you and Callie? Any wedding bells?"

Trevor choked on his coffee. When he finished sputtering, he said, "We're taking our time."

"I was just thinking that you and Tess might get a twofer."

"Like the Prescotts would ever let that happen," Owen said. "If you're smart, you'll do what my brother is doing. A destination wedding in Vegas. It's just close family and a few friends."

"That sounds wonderful," Tess said. "I wouldn't have to meet hundreds of people who don't matter. Or be afraid to wipe my mouth on a napkin that looks like it cost more than my dress."

"Miles doesn't strike me as a guy who wants all that crap," Trevor offered.

Tess sighed and shook her head. "It's not Miles. It's

his mom. He's the baby of the family, and this is his first marriage. It might be different if this were his second wedding, but not now."

"Good luck with that," Nina said. Turning back to Owen, she said, "You and Evelyn were mighty close at the engagement party." She waved a hand. "I mean more than usual."

"Like you were so quick to point out to Callie, we're always each other's date. We were having a good time."

"Mmm-hmm." She raised an eyebrow and gave him the once-over. "When was the last time you went on a real date?"

The change in subject caught him off guard. "Why?"

"Because it's been more than a year since we made a pact to get out there and date and look for real relationships. I see no movement on your end. Other than the dance you do with Evelyn."

"There was no pact. You just yelled at us. I never agreed to anything. I like my life just fine. I have everything I need." For the most part, it was true. Each branch of his life felt right. He loved his job. Working with the kids at the center gave him additional purpose. If he was horny, he knew women he could call. Every now and then, though, it seemed like something was missing. In those moments, he called Evelyn.

"I call bullshit."

"Yeah?" he countered. "Where's your serious relationship?"

"I'm working on it. I've been trying a lot of new experiences to put myself out there to meet people. You're not doing anything. You find some random woman to bang, and then you hang out with Evelyn."

"What's wrong with that?"

"What are you going to do when she finds someone else? Someone who will do everything you do, plus give her screaming good orgasms?"

His immediate reaction was to put his back up and declare that Evelyn wouldn't do that. She couldn't replace him. But the look on Nina's face told him the truth.

"She wants someone in her life." Nina's voice softened. "A partner in everything. You have to know that."

He swallowed nothing in an attempt to clear his throat. He didn't want things to change, but the thought of not having Evelyn in his life was painful.

Nina reached across the table and laid her hand over his. "If you don't make a move, you will lose her. Not completely. She'll still be there, just like we are. But it won't be the same, because she'll have what Tess and Miles do and what Trevor and Callie do. A life away from us and Sunny's Diner. That guy will be her first call when she has news about an award." She squeezed his fingers. "The look on your face says that you don't want that to happen."

What move am I supposed to make?

Trevor cleared his throat. "Leave him alone, Nina. You made your point." He made eye contact with Owen. "She doesn't know everything. Evelyn is happy. You're one of the most important people in her life. I can't imagine that ever changing."

"Yeah," Tess chimed in. "I mean, look how she remained friends with Donald all this time. She's moved on, but he's still part of her life."

Owen's stomach flipped. He did not want to be in

the same category as Evelyn's ex. Sure, she was friends with Donald, but it wasn't on the same level as what Owen shared with her.

He looked at Nina again. "Message received."

"What are you going to do?"

"Hell if I know." That was the God's honest truth. He stood and tossed money on the table. "I'll talk to you guys later. Don't call Evelyn about the nomination. Wait till she says something, okay?"

"Sure," Tess said. She touched his arm as he walked by. "It'll be fine. Don't let Nina scare you."

He nodded and headed out. He had a lot of thoughts to sort, so going for a run with Probie sounded like the best idea all morning.

EVELYN PACED IN HARRY'S OFFICE. HER COFFEE SLOSHED in her cup as she turned to walk the length again. "What time did you say they were making calls?"

"Soon," he answered without looking up from his computer.

Why call? It was an antiquated system. A mass email would be so much faster. She had a show to run. Anything would be better than standing in Harry's office. Waiting. It wasn't like they would call if she was being passed up again. How long was she supposed to wait?

Harry's phone rang, and she jumped. Turning to watch him as he answered, a boulder settled in her stomach. Then his face brightened. "Excellent. I'll let her know. Thank you."

He hung up and said, "I told you this was your year. You've got the nomination."

She almost dropped her coffee. Had she heard him right? "You said I got it?"

"Yeah. You're up for best producer. Your school shooting episode from last year."

Her heart stopped. Why couldn't one decent thing happen to her? She hated that episode. Dragging kids in to the studio to tell their story of watching their friends die while having gun-toting lobbyists talk about the right to bear arms had made her ill. Yeah, it had been their highest-rated episode ever, but she had despised every minute of it.

Harry stood in front of her. "What's wrong? You look like you're gonna be sick. This is great news. It's what you've always wanted."

"Yeah. I know." She inhaled deeply, shoving all unpleasant thoughts aside. *I did produce a kick-ass show.* "You're right. It's excellent news."

"Well deserved."

"Thanks." She gulped her now-lukewarm coffee. "Have you thought about my proposal for the new show? Now that I've got the nomination, pitching it to the network should be easier."

"I've looked it over. We'll see."

She hated when he offered that response. The lack of commitment drove her crazy.

"You know..." he started.

She set her cup down and waited.

"The anniversary of that episode is coming up."

No, she hadn't realized that. Mostly because she tried to block that entire situation from her memory.

"We should do a follow-up episode for the anniversary of the school shooting. Take it on location. Go to the school, see the kids, how they're doing a year later."

The coffee swirled in her stomach like acid, eating away at her. Rather than telling Harry to fuck off, she said, "I'll check the schedule, but for now, I have today's show to produce." Then she picked up her coffee cup and left his office.

For the rest of the day, Evelyn went through the motions of being a producer. She was on autopilot, telling cameras to shift, giving advice to Trent. Luckily, this episode was a follow-up. The guests had appeared at least once before for paternity testing and the people they thought were the fathers were not, in fact, the fathers. So now they were bringing in the next round of possible daddies.

Security was always on standby in case things got out of hand, but these guests leaned toward the weepy, not explosive. Although the men did jump around a bit in denial, no fights had to be broken up.

All of this allowed Evelyn to turn ideas over in her head. She'd thought having the nomination would be enough for Harry to at least run her idea up the ladder. Instead, he wanted more of that gut-wrenching stuff.

Her phone buzzed in her pocket with a text.

> Are we celebrating or commiserating tonight?

She wasn't sure how to answer Owen.

A little of both?

Huh?

I'll explain later.

Come to my house. I'll cook.

Evelyn immediately felt better. Owen didn't always cook, but when he did, it was yummy comfort food. Nothing fancy or elaborate for him. Chili, spaghetti, pot roast—things he'd learned to cook while at the firehouse.

As they moved to commercial break, Evelyn suddenly wondered if Owen ever cooked for anyone else. She'd mentioned to him a number of times what a turn-on it was for women to have a man cook for them. Did he add that to his repertoire for getting a woman in bed? Not that he needed help. Even if he weren't a good-looking guy, he had the whole firefighter-hero thing going for him.

Back from break, Evelyn watched the scene play out in front of her as Tiffany found out that she'd brought in the wrong man again and still didn't know who the father of her baby was. The dramatics unfolded on stage, and it had zero effect on Evelyn. She just didn't care.

Maybe doing a follow-up on the school shooting would be a good thing. At least she'd feel something.

OWEN STIRRED PASTA SAUCE ON THE STOVE AS JAZZ played in the background. His run with Probie had soothed his nagging thoughts from earlier. Evelyn's cryptic response left him wondering what happened with the nomination. Why would she need to both celebrate and commiserate?

In preparation, he planned a nice bottle of wine to celebrate and strawberry cheesecake with fresh whipped cream for dessert to commiserate. The spaghetti dinner would work for either a happy occasion or disappointment. As the water boiled, he added the pasta and then cut into the crusty bread to add butter and garlic before toasting it.

Just as he slid the garlic bread into the oven, Probie started dancing around, so he knew Evelyn was coming up the stairs. Although she had a key, he'd left the door unlocked for her. She pushed it open, which was Probie's invitation to rush through the house to get to her. The dog was still growing into his huge paws, so as he neared her and attempted to stop, he kind of skidded until he smacked into her legs.

"Hey, boy," she said in soothing tones as she bent to pet him. She rubbed her hands all over his sides and played with his ears.

Owen shook his head. She was going to have dog hair all over her expensive clothes. "Probie. Come on. Let's go out."

At the word "out," Probie scrambled back to Owen. Evelyn stood.

"I still think it's a crime you named that beautiful dog Probie. After a year, it's no longer probationary."

He turned to let the dog out the back door. "I told you when you gave him to me that it was permanent probation."

She'd gotten him the dog for his birthday last year, once he'd finished working on his house. She'd said the house needed a dog to make it feel like a home. He was convinced that she wanted a dog but didn't have the time to care for one. His house was the best of both worlds.

She followed him into the kitchen. "You'd no more get rid of that dog than you'd get rid of me."

He stirred the sauce again. "Probie fits him. He keeps screwing up and has a lot to learn. But no, I won't be getting rid of him." *Or you.*

She leaned over his shoulder and inhaled. "Mmm… pasta."

While she sniffed dinner, the scent of her perfume surrounded him, and her hair tickled his neck. She smelled better than anything he could put on a plate. So much for his head being clear. Nina's words dogged him.

Then Evelyn went to the sink and washed her hands, leaving him with nothing but the aroma of oregano and garlic.

"What can I help with?"

"Nothing. Pour yourself some wine and tell me what happened with the nomination."

She poured a full glass while he maneuvered around

the kitchen, draining the pasta and pulling the bread from the oven. Leaning against the table, she watched him prepare their plates.

"Are you going to keep me in suspense or what?"

"I got the nomination."

He set two full plates on the kitchen table and accepted the glass of wine she handed him. Clinking his glass against hers, he said, "Congrats?"

She smiled and sipped. "It's a good thing."

"But?"

"The nomination is for the episode I did on the school shooting last year."

"Damn." *What do I say to that?* His heart hurt for her. Evelyn's being upset over the nomination now made sense.

"Let's eat. This smells delicious."

They sat at the table and started eating.

"Your boss has to be thrilled with your nomination, right? I mean, it all looks good for them."

She lifted a shoulder and spun pasta on her fork. "Of course."

"Then why the long face?"

"Because right after we found out what the nomination was for, I asked Harry about my pitch for the new show, but he deflected. Then he reminded me that it's almost the anniversary of the shooting. As if I wanted or needed the reminder. He wants me to do a follow-up episode. Go to the school, visit with the kids. See how they're doing a year later."

"Fuck."

"Yeah." She stabbed at her noodles.

They ate in silence. Owen wished he could say

something to cheer her up, but when she'd come up with the idea for that episode, they'd fought a lot. He'd thought it was a bad idea. It was one thing to drag adults and their tragedy in front of an audience, but he firmly believed kids should be off-limits. And when it was over, he couldn't even say *I told you so* to her because the whole experience had torn her up.

After a while, he asked, "You're not going to do it, are you?"

She set her fork down and drained her glass of wine. "I don't have much of a choice."

"You always have a choice." He shoved some more pasta in his mouth, then reminded her, "You were miserable while working on that episode."

"I know."

"And it's not fair to the kids. To dredge up all that crap. What if they've started to get their lives back? They're going to remember the anniversary. They don't need someone shoving a camera in their faces and asking them about their dead friends." He thought of the few kids at the center who had been directly affected by the shooting. It had had a ripple effect, and all the other kids at the center had come in afraid and worried about when it would happen at their school.

Not if, but when.

"How can I say no if that's what they want? I can't just walk away from my career. I've worked really hard to get where I am."

He stood and put his plate in the sink. "You've already walked away. Ever since that episode, you've done almost nothing but who's-the-baby's-daddy shows. You stick to that because it's easy and predictable. It doesn't hit you emotionally."

"Easy and predictable aren't bad. Look at you," she said with a half-assed smile.

She always did her best to lighten the mood when things got rough, even if she wasn't feeling it. He didn't respond. The last thing he needed was Evelyn pointing out how boring he was.

"I'm kidding. Mostly." She kicked her smile up a notch.

Narrowing his eyes, he said, "I'm not always predictable." *Am I?*

She winked but didn't respond to his comment. "Going after that story was hard. But I ultimately have to do what my boss says."

"Your boss is a vulture." He took her plate and refilled her glass.

"It's the nature of the business."

"There's cheesecake in the fridge for dessert."

"Now who's spoiling whom? Cheesecake beats cheeseburgers any day." Her phone rang. Pulling it out, she said, "It's Donald. I'll be right back."

"Speaking of vultures," he said as she pressed the button to accept the call. She shot him a dirty look and walked toward the living room. Owen filled the sink to wash dishes. While he couldn't hear what Evelyn was saying to Donald, her voice changed when she talked to him. It was higher-pitched or too cheerful or something. It grated on his nerves.

He couldn't understand why she let the man stay in her life. For as long as he'd known Evelyn, she'd said that Donald hadn't done anything horrible in their marriage. He hadn't abused her or cheated on her. Their relationship had simply fizzled out. Owen never bought it. He thought they'd continued to sleep together when Donald was in Chicago. Then, within six months of the divorce, Donald had remarried.

The one night he and Evelyn had slept together had been on the heels of her getting the news that Donald had proposed to another woman.

And in the years since, Donald had blown into and out of her life, often after he went through a divorce or breakup. Owen never asked for particulars on the nature of their relationship, because he didn't like Donald. He didn't like who Evelyn was when Donald was around. While she shared that she'd spent time with her ex, Owen never asked if they'd slept together. He didn't want to know then, but now he was curious.

Instead of eavesdropping on her conversation, he turned up the jazz on his radio and washed dishes.

Chapter Three

Evelyn sat on the arm of Owen's couch.

"I'm so happy for you, Evie. The nomination is well deserved," Donald said.

She sighed. It didn't feel well deserved. Not for that episode. "Did you see the episode?"

"I saw clips from it. You did a great job."

He would think so. It had been his idea. As soon as the news reports had started coming in, Donald had called her at work and told her that if she wanted to take her career to the next level, this was the kind of story she needed to go after.

She'd listened to him the way she'd always listened to him. He'd been in the industry so many more years than she had. He knew what he was talking about and was rarely wrong. Didn't the nomination prove that he was right about this, too?

"Harry wants me to do it again," she said quietly, not wanting to rehash it with Owen.

"What do you mean?"

"It's almost the anniversary of the shooting."

"Oh, Evie, that's brilliant."

She bit her lip. Donald was right. In her gut, she knew it. But was an award worth the emotional cost?

"Have you thought about the angle? Have you reached out to the kids and the teachers? I wish I were in Chicago. I'd love to be a part of that. Even to just watch you work. It'll be amazing, Evie."

Donald kept talking as if it were a done deal. Like she shouldn't even consider not doing it. Then he abruptly switched topics to tell her what was going on in his life.

She let him ramble on for a few minutes about the news project he was on. It would be a series of night-time special events. While he droned, she stared at her feet. Kicking off her shoes, she ran her toes along the smooth, glossy hardwood. Between the low rumble of Donald's voice in her ear and the fact that she was caught up in her own head, she didn't hear Owen come into the room.

Suddenly a plate with a huge piece of cheesecake was thrust in front of her. She looked up, following the long, muscled arm with just enough hair to be inviting to touch, all the way to his face. He knew exactly what she needed when she needed it. What more could she ask for?

She didn't want to talk to Donald. He hadn't been the kind of husband who brought her cheesecake after a rough day. He'd wanted to tell her how to fix it. As if she didn't have a mind of her own.

"Hey, Donald? I have to go. Owen just placed a huge piece of cheesecake in front of me, and I can't be held responsible for the sounds that may come from my mouth momentarily." She accepted the plate from Owen with a smile.

Donald chuckled in her ear. "I remember how you are about cheesecake. Let me know if you want to bounce some ideas around for that follow-up."

As if she still needed him to guide her career. Years of therapy had taught her that she had been looking for a father figure because she'd had none growing up. She'd met him at work and without a doubt, it would be labeled harassment today, but back then, she'd been drawn to his power. He had taught her so much about being a producer. Which made him a pretty good mentor, but not a good husband. When she'd needed a partner, he'd told her to buck up and do what needed to be done to get where they wanted to go. Nothing was ever just about her.

"Okay. Thanks." She disconnected and slid onto the couch, thinking about her relationship with Donald. He was still good for shop talk, but he had no clue how to make her feel better. Hell, he didn't even understand that she was upset right now. That much hadn't changed over the years.

Owen sat next to her, the warmth of his body radiating across the short distance. This man, however, understood her. While he might not be the best talker, he was an excellent listener.

"What's up with Donald?"

"Why do you say his name like that?"

"Like what?"

"Like someone is stabbing your eyeball with a dull fork."

The corners of his mouth turned down. "I don't like him much."

Ha. That's an understatement. She didn't understand Owen's dislike of her ex. They'd met. Donald was always pleasant. Then again, Donald was pleasant with everyone. He viewed every introduction as the beginning of a possible future interaction.

She pointed at her cheesecake. "You're not having any?"

"I'm waiting for you to share."

"Why would I do that? You have a whole cake in there."

"But I don't want a whole piece. Just give me a bite."

She sighed, forked a piece, and held it out to him. He leaned forward and ate it. "Mmm... That is good."

"I gave you a bite. That's all you get." She shifted to move the plate out of his reach. The man had fast hands. "Anyway, to answer your question, Donald was calling to congratulate me." After another bite, she said, "He thinks I should do the follow-up on the shooting."

"Vulture," Owen mumbled as he pressed the button to turn on the TV.

"Can we not talk about it anymore? It's going to ruin this delicious dessert."

"One more thing and then I'll hand you the remote and you can pick whatever you want to watch." He twisted to look directly into her eyes.

Seemed like a fair trade-off, so she nodded.

"Don't do anything because someone else says you should. Do what's right for you—what will make you feel good."

That one statement summed up why she loved him

and why he had been so good for her since her divorce. The sincerity on his face caused a lump to form in her throat. Owen didn't manipulate. He wanted what was best for her. She nodded.

With their gazes locked, she caught onto the idea of feeling good. She fell into the warmth of his brown eyes. Her pulse ticked up like it had in her kitchen the night of Tess's engagement party. *Stop it. This is Owen.* She blinked, and the charged moment passed…again.

He handed her the remote, and while she flipped it over to choose a show, Owen reached around and snagged her plate. Before she could blink, he popped the last piece of cheesecake into his mouth.

"That wasn't fair."

He answered with a grin before setting the empty plate on the table.

Her complaint was half-hearted. She'd give Owen anything he asked for. She settled next to him, and his arm came around her shoulders like it always did. When did snuggling with him become the norm? She couldn't remember, because it all felt so easy and natural.

"You'll pay for that," she said and scrolled through the channels until she could find the silliest, sappiest romantic comedy possible.

The thing was, he didn't care. He let her lean on him and pretend life was light and happy. And for that, she loved him.

Owen was exhausted walking away from the firehouse to go home. His phone had been buzzing repeatedly, so he finally checked it. He'd missed a few calls and texts from Evelyn.

He'd forgotten to tell her that he was working overtime, but they hadn't had plans. He'd worked an extra half shift to cover for Joe, whose kid had some school performance. He hadn't counted on the last call being so bad. But it could've gone much worse. Pushing away the thoughts of how bad it could've been, he called Evelyn back.

She answered on the first ring. "Hey."

"Hey. I'm fine. I worked overtime for Joe."

The breath of her sigh was loud enough that he could imagine it brushing his cheek.

"What's up?" he asked. She rarely checked in on him while he was on duty. They texted during shift to chat, make plans for dinner, or talk about friends. She didn't ask about his calls. But when he had a hard day, like today, she always listened.

"Nothing. I just thought it was weird that I hadn't heard from you. You usually call or text when you get off shift to let me know you're okay."

"The last call was rough. Took a long time."

"But you're okay?"

"Yeah," he lied. Physically, he was fine. Emotionally, he needed distance to get a grip.

"Come over."

"I'm exhausted. I'll probably just crawl into bed. And I have to check on Probie." He had a neighbor who walked his dog when he was on shift, but Probie would be missing him by now.

"Are you sure?"

"Yeah. I'll call you tomorrow." He disconnected and waved as he walked through the firehouse. Outside the sun was low in the sky. He closed his eyes and stood for a minute, taking a long breath.

It was late. It always threw him off getting out any time other than first thing in the morning. He liked the routine. But when a buddy needed you to cover, you did. It was how a team worked.

He hadn't eaten in hours. His stomach had to be empty, but he didn't feel particularly hungry. He could make himself a sandwich before he went to bed. A cold beer sounded really good. Too bad he couldn't remember if he had any in the fridge. He'd been spending time at Evelyn's, so he wasn't sure if he'd finished what he'd had. Ever since she'd gotten the nomination a few weeks ago, she'd been working exceptionally long days trying to figure out what to do about the follow-up episode to the school shooting. They hadn't had a lot of time together, but it was enough that he hadn't paid attention to what was in his own fridge.

He didn't have the energy to stop at a store. If he was out of beer, he'd go without. At his car, he rolled down the windows and blasted the air-conditioning to flush out the stagnant heat. He waited outside the car while it cooled. Leaning against the back door, he looked up at the late-evening sun.

He closed his eyes against the glare. Images flashed in his mind of Jamal hanging onto the edge of the car leaning over the highway. He took a few deep breaths to erase the haunting pictures. Nothing would truly wipe them out, but he recounted every step they'd taken to save the victims of the car accident. Retraced his movements to verify that he'd done everything possible to keep his crew safe.

And ultimately, Jamal was safe. He'd be sore tomorrow, and would likely need a few days off, but he was fine.

Satisfied he'd done his best on the call, he climbed in his car and drove home. When he parked in front of his house, he saw Evelyn sitting on his steps.

With his bag in hand, he got out and asked, "What are you doing here?" Then realized he sounded like a dick. "I mean—"

She stood and waved at him. "I know what you mean. I wanted to check on you."

Still pushing thoughts away, he said nothing.

"I know you said you're fine. And physically, you might be."

She knew he would want to be alone. But Evelyn pushed past anything he said he wanted.

"I'm tired."

"And probably hungry because you didn't eat."

The corner of his mouth lifted. She knew him too well.

She stepped closer. "I already walked Probie. Dinner is on the table. Beer is in the fridge." Then she wrapped her arms around his neck and held him tight. "I'm glad you're okay," she whispered in his ear. "I don't know what I'd do without you."

He dropped his bag and folded both arms around her waist. The scent of her comforted him and brought out all the crap he'd shoved down since leaving the accident. Instead of letting go, he buried his face in her hair and held her tighter until the flood of emotion passed.

Evelyn ran her hand over his head, soothing him without saying a word. God, how he'd missed having someone to come home to after a shift like this. To be able to lose himself in another person. For a few minutes, they stood like that. When he finally had himself together, he pulled back.

"The neighbors are gonna talk," he said gruffly.

She smiled. "It's about time you gave them something to talk about." She patted his chest. "Don't forget to eat."

When she backed away, he caught her wrist. "Come inside."

"I thought you were tired."

"I am. You can keep me company while I eat the dinner you brought. Hope it's something good."

"Nothing but the best for you, of course." She pushed the front door open, and Probie danced around to greet him. He tossed his bag in the corner and bent to pet his dog.

"You want to eat in the kitchen or in here?" Evelyn asked.

"In here. I just want to collapse."

She nodded toward the couch. "Have a seat. I'll grab the food."

He plopped on the couch and kicked off his shoes. Probie moved in a circle and settled at his feet. Evelyn came back into the room with a giant salad and a bottle of beer.

"I figured you'd want something light before bed."

"Anything would be great. Thanks." He took the salad, balanced it on his lap, and took a long swig of ice-cold beer.

"Are you going to tell me what happened?" she asked as she joined him on the couch.

"No."

"I won't freak out. I know your job is dangerous, but I trust you to do everything you can to make it back to me." She reached over and held his hand. The gesture was the same as always, yet different. When she was so understanding, eager for him to unburden, it was difficult to keep the distance he so desperately needed. Stacy had never been able to handle hearing about his job. She definitely couldn't handle him after a call like today. He wanted to forget, but he'd learned it was too much to expect from someone else.

Except Evelyn made him feel safe enough to talk. She could handle it. He set his food on the table.

"We had a bunch of calls today. A small kitchen fire and three car accidents. On the last call, we were pulling victims from a smashed car. The vehicle had flipped and was stuck against the guardrail." He stared at his hands in his lap. Evelyn still held one, but his other was clenched in a white-knuckled fist. He slowly opened his fingers and forced them to relax. "Jamal almost slid off the side of the car and over the rail. He could've fallen into traffic below. I grabbed him, and the rest of the guys pulled us all to safety."

"Jamal's okay?"

"Yeah." Telling her hadn't been as hard as he'd thought. Tension eased from his shoulders as she stroked the back of his hand.

"I'm glad."

She showed no signs of wariness or concern over his job. No hint of needing to get away. For the first time in hours, he breathed freely.

This was what it meant to have someone in your corner. Emotion clogged his throat and pricked the back of his eyes, so he took a swig of beer.

To her credit, Evelyn pretended not to notice, turning on the TV. She talked over the top of everything, recalling what craziness had happened on set the last few days. She did everything she could to distract him and keep him from feeling like crap. It was weird not having to comfort someone else. Evelyn just took care of him.

He finished his beer and his salad, stretched his legs out, and pulled her close. They spent a lot of time like this. It was something he didn't want to lose.

She flipped through channels again—it drove him crazy that she had a hard time settling on something.

The conversation from Sunny's came back to him. Between that and his own slight brush with mortality, he wanted reassurance. "Are you dating anyone?"

"Huh?" She looked up at him over her shoulder.

"Dating? Are you?"

"You know I'm not."

"I know you don't have a boyfriend. But are you looking?"

"I don't know. I told you I'm not actively on the hunt." She twisted her body to face him. "Why?"

"Just wondering. We talk about pretty much everything, but you haven't mentioned any dates in a while."

"Haven't had much success."

"Oh."

"Is there a reason you're asking?"

"Just curious." It wasn't totally the truth, but he didn't have a better answer. What was he supposed to say? He was a selfish bastard who didn't want to lose her to someone else, but he wasn't sure if he wanted to change their relationship. What if he made a move and it wasn't what she wanted? Things would get awkward.

And if she was open to changing their relationship? What else would change? Would they lose the ease they had with each other?

Early on, he and Stacy had been easy together. Then the stress of his job had taken its toll. She wanted more of everything, and he hadn't been enough. How could he be enough for Evelyn?

She gave him an odd look and then turned back to the TV. He leaned against the back of the couch, closed his eyes, and listened to her running commentary.

Right now, they each played a role in each other's life. If they changed that, he might lose everything. He could be a difficult partner. What if she couldn't handle this side of him 24-7? He'd prefer to play it safe and keep the Evelyn he had right now.

Evelyn knew as soon as Owen slipped off to sleep. She should have left, but something told her to stay. He needed her, even if he wouldn't say it. It was more than having someone to make sure he ate dinner. He hated to lean on anyone, so sometimes she needed to just push up against him until he had no choice. This evening had been the first time she truly considered the dangers of his job. She obviously understood the danger, and he'd shared enough stories over the years for her to know how it affected him.

She just wanted to be here for him. Instead of waking him to go to bed, she continued to snuggle against him on the couch.

Which was exactly where she found herself the following morning. She slowly stretched. At some point, they'd shifted, and Owen was fully beneath her. His morning hard-on greeted her and she slid away. Normal biological function or not, she didn't need to think about Owen's dick being hard.

She shuffled to the kitchen to make coffee. Then she went to the bathroom to shower. She'd spent the night at Owen's before, and he'd slept at her place, too. But something about last night had felt different. Her brain was foggy, and she couldn't quite decipher what had changed. Water sluiced over her, and she sighed. Owen had a great shower.

He'd offered to redo her bathroom and put in the same fixtures, but it wouldn't be the same.

A thump sounded at the door. "Hey." His voice was sleep-rough. "I'm coming in. I gotta piss."

"Such a charming guy. Do you treat all your overnight guests like this?"

"Nope. You're special."

She washed her hair and pretended that the rough sound of his voice had no effect on her. He took care of business and left without another word.

Why had she thought something was different about last night? What kind of fantasy was she trying to spin in her head? She smiled at her silliness and rinsed off. Maybe Owen was making a point last night by asking her if she was dating. Maybe he was subtly hinting.

She turned off the water and wrapped a towel around herself. Maybe it was time to create online profiles again… but that took so much effort. Last summer when Nina had challenged them all to get out and try to find relationships, Evelyn had. She'd rejoined at least three dating sites.

It was so tedious, though. Guys wanted to text and chat forever, but never got around to asking her out. When she did the asking, it never went further than a drink. She had better things to do than waste time on guys when it wouldn't go anywhere.

As she dried off, she realized she hadn't thought about what to wear. Owen knocked again. Then the door cracked open and one arm snaked through holding a T-shirt and shorts.

"Thanks."

"I want them back."

"Yeah, yeah." She took the pile and pulled the clothes on.

"I'm serious," he continued through the crack in the door. "I bet if I rummage through your closet, I'll find a third of my clothes."

She opened the door. "A third is an exaggeration."

"Not by much." He eyed her up and down. "But you might look better in them than I do."

She smiled. "Good to know."

In the kitchen, Owen poured them both a cup of coffee. "What do you have going on today?"

"The usual Sunday stuff—laundry, grocery shopping. Then I might go into the studio to work on the show for a bit."

"Isn't that what your regular workweek is for?"

"When I'm there during the week, my time is filled with phone calls and meetings, and then we're filming. I think I have an angle for the school shooting follow-up."

"Does that angle involve not doing it?"

She sighed. "I told you I can't just not do it. But I have ideas I think I can live with."

"Tell me."

"I'm not ready to talk about it yet. I have to make sure it'll work. What're you doing?"

"I have a basketball game at the center. The middle school girls' team is on fire. They keep playing the way they are, and they'll have scouts looking at them as soon as they hit high school."

She watched his face bloom with happiness. The kids at the center brought so much joy to his life. He'd make such a great dad. "Why don't you have kids?"

He choked on his coffee.

Her question was a little abrupt, but given his questioning last night, she figured it was open game.

"I kind of need a woman for that to happen."

"But do you want them?"

He slowly licked his lips. "I did at one point. I was sure Stacy and I would have at least a couple. But it didn't happen. In the meantime, life kept going. Now I wouldn't be upset if I met someone and she had kids or wanted to, but I'm not searching for it anymore. Not like I did when I was younger."

"You'd be an excellent dad. I see it in your face every time you talk about the kids at the center."

"I get my fill there. I get to be a friend and mentor to a lot of kids, but I don't have to do it twenty-four-seven. I still get my life the way I want it. It's the best of both worlds."

She sipped her coffee. "You don't think you're missing out on not having your own?"

"Do you?"

"Hell no. I'm not made to be a mom. A cool aunt, sure. But making my life revolve around someone needy and dependent wouldn't work for me." Yet another reason she wouldn't date someone younger. She wanted someone on the same page. Someone who would respect her career. Someone who wouldn't pressure her for kids.

He drank his coffee and didn't say anything else on the topic. She couldn't read his expression. They'd been friends for so long, she couldn't remember if they'd ever had this conversation before. Maybe early on when they were both thinking about dating again and looking for a partner. His answer now surprised her. She wasn't sure she totally believed him. Part of her wondered if he just gave up on the idea of having his own kids so he was selling himself on being satisfied with what he had.

She finished her coffee and put her cup in the sink. "What time is the game?"

"Three."

"Maybe I'll stop by."

"You don't like basketball."

"But I like watching you coach." She'd come to watch many sporting events simply because it was important to him. "If you win, I might even buy you dinner."

"I think I owe you dinner for last night." He stood next to her and took her hand. "Thanks for everything."

"I didn't do much."

"You gave me what I didn't even know I needed. It was good to have company after a day like that."

"You would've done the same for me." And had many times.

"Thank you anyway." He kissed her temple.

The gesture was so sweet, she couldn't form words. She simply nodded. Stepping away, she scooped her hair up into a ponytail. "Don't forget the awards ceremony is Saturday. You're still coming, right?"

"Why wouldn't I?"

"Because I'm doing the follow-up show."

"I might not like parts of your job or how you choose to approach things, but I wouldn't miss that. It's important to you."

"Thanks. Black tie," she added.

"That was shady. Getting a confirmation before reminding me that I have to wear a penguin suit."

She stepped closer again and patted his chest. "You make a good penguin, though."

"Whatever."

"See you later." She gave Probie a quick belly rub and left. Unease settled in. Things felt different with Owen, but she couldn't quite put her finger on it. They'd always been comfortable around each other, regardless of what was going on in their lives. It wasn't so much discomfort as a kind of shift. She just didn't know if she should do anything about it.

OWEN ARRIVED AT THE CENTER EARLY BECAUSE HE LIKED to have time to hang out with the kids before warm-ups. He strode through the door and hadn't gotten more than five steps into the hallway before Sandra called to him from her office.

The woman who was normally bright and bubbly looked beat.

"Hi, Sandra. What's up?"

"I know you have a game to get ready for, but I wanted to give you a heads-up. The budget isn't looking good. If we don't get a sizable influx of donations by the end of the year, we're going to have to cut hours and programs."

He sank to the seat in front of her desk. They'd had this conversation many times over the years, but he couldn't remember a time when Sandra looked so defeated. "Where do you even start? How do you decide what to cut?"

"I don't know." She shook her head sadly. "Unstructured things like open gym hours will probably go first. Paying to keep the doors open and lights on when we don't know how many kids will utilize it doesn't make sense."

"But it's a safe haven for them. They know we're here and they have options. It keeps them out of trouble."

"I know, but I certainly don't want to cut classes or teams. They offer the best ROI."

He was sickened by the thought of having to think of return on investment in relation to his kids.

"Let's host some more benefits or fund-raisers. If people knew what we do, they'd give more."

"We're going to try. Thank you for all your help. I don't know what I'd do without you. I wish I could offer you a salary."

"I don't need money. I love being here." Unlike being a firefighter, working here allowed him to see the long-term positive effects of what he did. Sure, he saved lives, but once a fire was out, he rarely found out what happened to the survivors. At the center, he watched kids grow into adults.

"And we all appreciate it."

He stood. "I'm headed to the gym to set up for the game. Will you be there?"

"No way would I miss our girls winning. They've become quite the team."

"They have a lot of talent."

"Talent only gets you so far. You've taught them discipline and self-confidence. That will take them far in life."

He certainly hoped so. He grabbed his bag and went to the gym. Unsurprisingly, a group of girls were already there, suited up in their worn and tired uniforms, scrolling through their phones, and laughing at whatever silliness they saw on the screens.

On the other side of the gym, parents were setting up a table to sell concessions, one of their smaller fund-raisers. He waved at them as he walked to the sidelines and set down his bag. Looking at the girls, he asked, "Keisha, is Malik going to be here today?"

Keisha's older brother had been coming to most practices, acting as an unofficial equipment manager.

"Here, Coach," he heard from behind him before Keisha could even answer.

Tall and lanky, Malik ran up to him. The boy wore basketball shorts the same color as the girls' uniforms. Owen tossed him the keys to the equipment room. "Roll out the balls and then fill the water bottles."

"Gotcha."

Owen hadn't been looking for an assistant, but Malik had been a godsend. He ran around doing the things Owen often postponed or neglected. A few minutes later, the girls were standing around him, phones put away. They were ready for warm-ups, but first, they wanted to know the scoop on the opposing team. It was something he'd been trying to do this season. He visited other teams and watched them play. It gave him valuable insight into how to strategize. A side benefit was that sharing the information with the girls sometimes eased their minds and nerves.

Knowing what was coming was usually better than the unknown. Even if the team had a reputation for being better than them, Owen could find something for his girls to feel better about. Maybe their center couldn't jump as high, or their forward had a weak layup. Even the small things could give them positive vibes.

"This team is good. It won't be a walk in the park today, so I hope you're all well-rested."

"Shoot. Is it ever a walk in the park?" Lia asked.

He chuckled. "One thing I want to warn you about is their audience. I went to an away game to watch them play and they had fans—a lot of fans—cheering and jeering loudly. Don't let them get to you."

Malik returned pushing the bin of balls. "I think we got that covered tonight."

Owen turned to look at him. Malik lifted his chin to point toward the gym entrance. There was a line of people waiting to get in to watch the game. At first glance, it looked like at least half of them were wearing their team colors. They normally had a decent turnout of parents and friends at games to cheer the girls on, especially since they'd been winning. But the line at the door was beyond the norm.

"How?" Owen asked.

"You should know by now, Coach, that we have big mouths. Word spreads. You're not the only one who can do some recon."

Sure enough, as the girls started their drills, middle school and high school boys were leading the way to show people where to sit for the game. The opposing team arrived, and Owen introduced himself. Sandra came through with a smile and a nod. She greeted each of the girls by name and wished them good luck.

By the time they were ready to start the game, the bleachers were filled, and Malik was adding chairs along the walls. The cheering was thunderous when his team scored their first basket. He had a hard time calling out directions past the lump in his throat. This was proof of why the center was so important to the neighborhood.

As Keisha broke away dribbling down center court, a flash of movement by the door caught his eye. He looked toward the entrance. Evelyn was here. She didn't come to games too often. She wasn't into sports. But she came to support him. She tried to find a spot on the bleachers, but ultimately just ended up standing.

The whole time he coached, he was keenly aware of her presence. She wasn't a distraction, really. It was more like he wanted to show her that he was okay after the call yesterday at work. If he could show her that the call didn't affect him as much as she thought, they would go back to normal.

She'd caught him in a weak moment last night, and he'd needed her presence to recover from what had happened. He didn't like relying on other people to feel better. He'd always managed to get his shit together on his own after a tough call. But last night, when Evelyn was standing in front of him, concerned for his well-being, he was hit with a strong urge to seek comfort from her.

Which was totally inappropriate.

So he'd coach the hell out of this game to show her yesterday was no big deal. He didn't need her to worry about him. Because doing so might irrevocably change their relationship.

EVELYN WASN'T EVEN COMPLETELY SURE WHAT CAUSED her to show up at Owen's basketball game. She didn't like sports, but after last night, part of her wanted to make sure he was okay. She'd never seen him so shaken up by a call at work. Then again, she rarely knew about the tough calls. It finally occurred to her that Owen typically avoided her after a call like that.

Which made her wonder how he handled it.

Bottling up that much emotion was not healthy. But watching him coach in this ear-splittingly loud gym was nothing short of amazing. The yelling and screaming might give her a headache, but it didn't seem to affect Owen or his team at all.

She understood some of the rules of basketball, so she could follow what the girls were doing, but when Owen was waving his hands and yelling what she assumed were directions, she couldn't hear him and had no idea what it all meant. When a girl from the other team practically ran over one of Owen's girls, he rushed to the court to check on her. After she stood, looking no worse for the wear—and offering the offending girl a nasty glare—Owen turned on the ref and the opposing coach. He was not having any of it.

She still couldn't hear what he was saying, but in her head, his voice rang clear as he stood up for his player.

Evelyn had never had a thing for athletes, or coaches, for that matter, but watching this side of Owen was pretty hot. His protective streak was more of a turn-on than she'd expected. For the rest of the game, she spent more time watching him than she did the players. Occasionally, he looked over and smiled at her. He was back to normal, the Owen she could always count on, with no sign of the distress from yesterday. Maybe she was blowing it all out of proportion.

Owen and his girls won the game in the last few seconds. The crowd went wild, and Owen's team surrounded him. They took a few minutes to high-five with big smiles before he pointed them in the direction of the other team, who were lined up to congratulate them.

As she watched the entire thing play out, Evelyn realized that this was yet another family that Owen had created for himself. He had pockets of people who cared about him everywhere. *How exactly do I fit in?*

Jamal had told her that she was one of them, but she wasn't. His family treated her like she was one of them, but she wasn't. And the kids at the center were completely removed from her. She and Owen were best friends, but what exactly did that mean? He talked about the kids, so she was familiar with them, but she didn't have a place here.

She was so lost in her own thoughts that she didn't notice Owen coming up on her. Suddenly she was being swept off her feet in a big circle.

"I'm glad you made it. This was a big win."

"Congratulations. It was an awesome game." She patted his shoulder. "You can put me down now."

The look on his face said he hadn't considered how his display would appear to everyone else. He took her hand. "Come for pizza with us to celebrate?"

"You sure?"

"About what? Pizza? Pizza is the best way to celebrate with kids—cheap and easy. They eat a lot."

"No," she answered with a smile. "I mean about me tagging along. Shouldn't you be hanging with your team?"

"Of course you can eat with us. Most of the families are coming. You're my family."

For a guy who didn't like to talk much, his words smoothed out the questions and concerns that had been bouncing around in her head for the last hour.

She might not have much of her own family, but if Owen was willing to share his, she'd take it.

FRIDAY MORNING, OWEN GOT OFF WORK AND TOOK A nap before going to pick up his rented tuxedo. If Evelyn kept dragging his ass to these fancy events, he might have to invest in a tux of his own. Normally, on Fridays, Evelyn tried to get off work a little early, but with the award ceremony and the follow-up episode, she'd said she was going to work late.

He hadn't seen her since she'd stopped by to watch

the basketball game. He'd loved having her with him and the team when they'd gone out for pizza, but he missed his time alone with her. He texted her to see if she wanted to go out for dinner tonight.

As much as I'd love to, I can't.

Working late?

Yeah, but then I'm meeting a friend for drinks.

A friend. No name. That burrowed into Owen's nerves. Evelyn had a date.

Okay. Have fun. See you tomorrow.

See you then.

The conversation irritated Owen in an irrational way. He knew Evelyn dated. She'd said as much. But then she said she wasn't actively looking. What the heck was this then? And why not just say she had a date?

He flipped through the contacts in his phone. He had women to call. Tara was usually up for a good time. He scrolled to her name and paused. There was a reason why he'd said no to plans with Tara to be with Evelyn.

He wasn't a hundred percent sure what that reason was, but it was there. Tara was sexual release with little emotional connection. She was nice, but there was nothing else there.

Evelyn was everything else.

Which was why her date tonight irritated him. He

felt like they'd been working toward something. Something that would make her dating bug him. They obviously weren't on the same page.

Instead of a hookup, he opted to go for a run with his other best friend. Probie scrambled as soon as he heard the leash. He knelt and rubbed his dog. "Yeah, boy. Who needs women?"

After a three-mile run, Owen didn't feel any better. He was still thinking about women. First, Evelyn, wondering what was happening on her date. Then Nina and all the things she'd said about Evelyn. How Evelyn would never be satisfied living life like he did. She would want the whole package with one guy.

He took a quick shower and called his brother. "Want to go out for a few beers?"

"Uh...it's Friday night."

"Yeah. So?" He paused. "Wait. Does Alicia tie up all of your Friday nights because you're about to get married? Doesn't she know she has a whole lifetime for that?"

Dave laughed. "Alicia's not even home. She's having a girls' night."

"Then what's the problem?"

"There is no problem. I figured if you weren't working, you'd either be on a date or with Evelyn."

Owen grunted. "I do have more to my life than getting laid and hanging out with Evelyn."

"Really? Have you started doing those things together? 'Cause that would free up some time."

"No. I'm not sleeping with my best friend." Why does everyone think he and Evelyn should be fucking? "Do you want to go out or not?"

"Tell me where."

They met up at a sports bar in between their houses. Although they saw each other pretty often, it was usually at family things. Especially since he'd proposed to Alicia. Owen missed hanging out with his brother.

"How are the wedding plans?" he asked.

Dave shrugged. "Alicia is doing all the planning. She just tells me where to send the money."

"It's your wedding, too."

"The wedding is important to her. I'd be happy with a judge and my family."

"I thought she was keeping it small."

"She thought by making it a destination wedding, it would be small. But word travels, and people want to come to the wedding and turn it into a vacation."

"How many people?"

"Still not huge. I think she said fifty?" They sat in silence for a while, watching the baseball game on the huge TVs.

"What's on your mind?" Dave asked.

"What do you mean?"

"I like seeing you, but it's not like you to call to have beers. You obviously have something you want to talk about or ask me, so out with it."

"As someone with a semi-objective opinion, why do you think my marriage to Stacy didn't work?"

"Because she cheated on you," Dave said as if Owen had lost every brain cell in his body.

"I don't need you to state the obvious. But it didn't just happen. Obviously, something was lacking. I didn't see the signs." He took a drink of beer. Then added, "And don't question my skills in the bedroom. I've never had any complaints."

Dave shook his head. "Stacy was...I don't know... flighty? Insecure? You were gone a lot. She didn't know what to do with herself. A person can only do so much sitting around waiting and wondering."

Owen thought about it. Back then, he'd taken on every extra shift he could. He'd wanted to provide them with a good life. Stacy had complained about the hours he put in on the job. He just kept promising that it wouldn't be forever. Maybe if she'd had her own things to do... Besides another man. But when he was around, she'd complained they hadn't done exciting stuff together. He'd had enough excitement at work, so at home he wanted calm.

No matter what he did, it hadn't been enough. At every turn, he'd felt like a failure. He'd wanted to give Stacy everything, but he couldn't quite get there.

He'd never talked about work, because it made her worry too much. They didn't have hobbies together. Outside of sex, the connection hadn't been there. Had he not tried hard enough to forge that connection?

"What made you think about that?" Dave asked, bringing him back to the present.

"Something a friend mentioned. She said that Evelyn would want to get married again, or at least have a serious relationship. It got me wondering why I haven't found one."

"You haven't tried."

He couldn't argue that point. Early on after the divorce, he had, but since he'd forged his friendship with Evelyn, not really.

"I like my life. It's full. I have sex when I want it. I

have a great job and good friends. I love my time at the youth center."

"Companionship. If you're getting it from your friends, maybe you don't need the serious relationship."

He remembered what Evelyn said about having someone to come home to. Right now, when he felt that need, she was there. But for how long?

Chapter Four

All day Saturday, Evelyn worked with a bundle of nerves rolling in her stomach. The damn awards ceremony shouldn't matter. She'd never even been nominated before, so that should be enough, but it wasn't. She wanted to win, but she wished it were for any other episode. All week, they'd been looking at footage from last year's show as she tried to decide what would work for part of the follow-up.

She'd been tight-lipped around Harry, not wanting him to shoot her ideas down. Trent, the show's host, was on board with whatever she told him to do. He was easy to work with, so she couldn't complain about him, per se. But she didn't particularly like him, either. She didn't know what was wrong with her lately. Nothing fit quite right.

Stepping into her sleek black gown, she worried she might not be able to zip it up. Everything in her life was a little off. A knock sounded as she slid into her heels, the back of her dress still gaping. A second later, the door opened, and Owen came in.

Damn he looks good in a tux.

"Wow. You're ready?"

"Just about. You don't have to look so shocked. I left the studio early to make sure I was on time." In fact, Harry had shoved her out the door early in the afternoon. It was as if no one trusted her to show up as scheduled.

He looked her up and down, the sensation raking across her nerves, setting them on fire.

"You look amazing."

"Thanks. You're not so bad yourself. Can you zip me up?" She turned her back to him.

He tugged at the material, and she instinctively sucked in. They were silent as he slid the zipper up, his fingers grazing her skin. When it neared the top, he paused and swept her hair to the side. He stepped closer, close enough that his breath caressed her neck as he clasped the top.

Her dress was completely fastened, but neither of them moved. His hands felt so natural on her body. Fuck. She had to stop thinking like that.

Stepping away, she stuffed her purse with her phone, keys, ID, and some cash.

"How was your date last night?"

She paused at the question. "What date?"

"Late drinks?"

"Oh, that. It wasn't a date. I told you I was meeting a friend."

He looked at her with a raised brow.

"A friend. That wasn't code for a fuck buddy. Grant

was an assistant producer on Trent Talks for the first couple of years. He moved on, and we haven't seen each other in a long time. He wanted to meet for a drink. It was only one drink. I didn't get there till late. We caught up. Then I came home. Alone." Why did she feel like she was defending her social life to Owen?

Her explanation made him look relieved. Which was even more bizarre than her needing to defend her choices. What the hell was going on with them?

"How long does this thing go tonight?" he asked.

"Like eleven-ish? Why?"

"Just curious. I'm guessing that since you're nominated this year, you'll want to stay for the whole thing."

In past years, they'd always cut out early and found decent food to eat to make up for whatever rubber chicken banquet food they'd been served. "Let's play it by ear. If I don't win, I'll be ready to leave early."

He tugged at his tie and crooked his elbow for her to take. "Hmm. Now I don't know which is worse—to wish you don't win so we can leave early or wish that you do, knowing I'll be stuck there all night."

She took his arm. "There's a stocked bar."

"I can't drink too much. I'm working tomorrow."

"Party pooper."

He led her from the condo to his car. They drove to the banquet in silence, Evelyn's nerves increasing with each passing mile.

"You okay?" Owen finally asked as he pulled up to the valet stand.

"Nervous. I've always wanted the nomination, but I never considered how nerve-racking it would be."

The valet opened her door. A moment later, Owen

took her hand. "You'll be fine." Having him in her corner made her believe it. Inside the hall, they found their table, where they'd be sitting with everyone else from Trent Talks. Although this award was small compared to the Emmys, it was well-attended, with a few famous faces milling around.

She grabbed champagne from the first tray she could find. Then she led Owen through the throngs of people to decide who she wanted to talk to. Over the course of the week, she'd spent some time reviewing other executive producers who might be interested in her pitch. She'd enjoyed working with Harry, but she wasn't about to let her career stagnate. She was ready for something different.

She barely made it five steps when she heard Owen grunt. When she turned to see what the problem was, Donald came up to her, arms open wide.

"Donald? What are you doing here?"

"You think I'd miss this, Evie?" He folded her into his arms, pulling her hand from Owen's in the process. "I'm so proud of you."

Over Donald's shoulder, she saw Owen cross his arms on his chest. Being in her ex's embrace offered nowhere near the warmth she'd had holding Owen's hand. She forced a smile at Owen that she hoped was apologetic.

When Donald released her, she reached over and pulled Owen close. "You remember Owen, don't you?"

Donald extended a hand. "Of course. The firefighter, right?"

Owen nodded. His hand hesitantly came across and shook Donald's.

Instead of addressing the tension between the men, she said, "I think I have the follow-up to the shooting episode solved. I've got a lineup of experts who can talk about the long-term effects of such trauma. I've got a few staff members who can talk about how the school is different now. I think it'll work. But don't say anything to Harry yet. I want to get parts filmed before he shoots the idea down."

"Evie, of course he's going to shoot that down. You need to bring the kids in. Nothing will have the emotional impact kids do."

Owen flinched beside her.

"I can't do that to those kids," she said quietly.

"If you want to make your mark, sweetie, you need to go big. Someone is going to run the story. Why not you?"

Because it'll make me feel dirty. "I'll think about it."

She looked past Donald and added, "There are some people I want to talk to. See you later."

Turning away, Owen was at her side. "Why the hell do you do that?"

"Do what?"

"Look for his approval. You're good at what you do. You don't need his input."

"I wasn't looking for his approval."

"Oh yeah? Then why is he the only person you talked to about your plans for the show? I asked you to tell me and I got nothing. He didn't even ask. You just jumped, fawning all over him."

She pulled him to a stop. "I don't fawn over anyone. Donald is a heavy hitter in this industry. He knows what works and what doesn't. I respect his opinion."

"Looks like more than respect."

"What's that supposed to mean?" She drained her glass and grabbed another from a passing waiter.

His face was stony. "Whenever you talk to him or he's around, you turn into a simpering little girl."

Her hand tightened on the glass, and she tensed every muscle to prevent herself from dumping the champagne over his head.

As if he knew what she was thinking, his face softened. His palm came to her face. "You are a beautiful, strong woman who can take on anything. I hate that he makes you doubt yourself. You don't need him."

She wanted to stay mad, but something about the look in his eyes melted her. He was always in her corner no matter what.

"Please don't be mad at me. I'm not trying to piss you off. I don't like him. And I despise when he calls you Evie, like some little girl."

Taking a deep breath, she said, "You don't have to like him. And I don't simper around him. Hell, I don't ever simper. As far as the nickname goes, when we met, I sometimes used it. I no longer do."

As she spoke, her back straightened and she felt more like herself.

"There she is." He took his hand away from her face with a smile.

Just like that, they were back to normal. It was one of the many things she loved about her relationship with him. They could say anything to each other and be okay.

"It's almost dinnertime. Let's go back to the table."

He looked confused. “I thought there was someone you wanted to talk to.”

“Nope. I wanted to get away from Donald.”

He chuckled, and they wound their way back to their table.

She didn’t want to think about whether Owen had a point about her relationship with Donald. She and Donald had remained friends after the divorce. She never knew when they might cross paths professionally, and she couldn’t afford to appear to be difficult to work with. Since she didn’t have any hard feelings—at least not in many years—there was no reason they couldn’t be friends.

When her marriage had ended, it was mostly because she’d felt like it was a business relationship. Donald had always pushed her to do more, meet more people, get more exposure. He’d acted like a business manager more than a husband, so they’d grown apart. That had been bad enough, but her anger had come when Donald had moved on to someone else, and from the outside, it’d appeared she had everything Evelyn had wanted.

It wasn’t until years later, after Donald’s second divorce, that Evelyn realized that Donald didn’t have it in him to be a husband, a true supportive partner. But he was a pretty good friend to have in this business.

As they took their seats, Evelyn introduced Owen to Harry and his wife, as well as the others at the table. Unless someone from their station was nominated, Harry rarely attended the ceremony. She couldn’t remember if Owen had met him before. It didn’t take long before Harry was on her again about the follow-up.

She tensed and took another sip of champagne. "We film this week. I'll send you something as soon as I have it. It'll be ready to air on the anniversary. Have I ever missed a deadline?"

"Well, no," Harry blustered. Under the table, Owen placed a hand on her knee, a silent show of support. She shot him a quick smile of thanks. For the rest of the meal, people made small talk about current events and the state of the city. Just as she relaxed, the emcee stepped to the mic and began the awards ceremony.

Evelyn realized that she should've eaten more of the rubber chicken because the alcohol in her stomach was gearing up for revolt with each passing moment.

OWEN SAT SILENTLY, FEELING HELPLESS AS HE WATCHED Evelyn. She wasn't herself at all tonight, and he didn't know how to help her. She shifted in her seat to fully face the stage, and Owen draped his arm around the back of her chair. She leaned into his shoulder.

They started giving out awards, and everyone politely clapped. In the past, she'd offered comments on each nominee and winner, complete with snark. Tonight, she sat like a robot. He leaned forward and whispered in her ear, "I'd pay fifty bucks for someone to break out in bad karaoke right now."

Evelyn snorted and slapped a hand over her mouth.

He tilted his chin toward the stage. "He looks like a guy who could really belt out 'All By Myself.' No wait. Even better, 'All Out of Love.'"

Her shoulders shook, and he knew he'd accomplished what he'd wanted. She was relaxing.

She leaned back, her lips brushing his cheek as she said, "Love me some Air Supply."

He stared into her eyes. "I'll be sure to play some on the ride home."

"Thank you."

"It's why you brought me. Comic relief."

"You're way more than comic relief. I don't know what I'd do if you weren't here."

His chest tightened as he considered the weight of what they were to each other. He wouldn't want her to be here with some other man. This was his place. But he only said, "You'd handle it."

"I'd probably be puking in the corner."

"You start puking, you're on your own."

More applause engulfed the room, and they returned their attention to the stage. Through the next three awards, they whispered karaoke suggestions for each presenter and nominee. Then it was time for the producer award.

As they flashed clips of each episode on a big screen, Evelyn stiffened again. Color drained from her face. He took her hand as they made their way through each nominee.

When the presenter called her name, Evelyn didn't move. A spotlight swung to their table, and he squinted. She was frozen. With a nudge, he said "Hey, babe. You won."

His words got her moving. She stood and went to the stage to accept the award. As the applause died, she spoke quietly into the mic. Her eyes found his even with the bright lights blazing down on her. He swelled with pride.

"Thank you for this. I almost don't have words for how much this means." She pulled out a slip of paper and held it up. "Luckily, I came prepared."

The audience chuckled, but Owen saw the slight flutter of her hands. "I'm proud of the work I do," she continued. "This episode was, hands down, the most difficult thing I've ever done in this industry. It was a story that needed to be told, but I wish it wasn't possible to tell. No one, especially children, should have to experience this kind of trauma." She held up the glass statue. "I'd gladly give this up to never have to witness such tragedy again." She looked over the crowd. "As people, we have to do better. Thank you."

She left the stage, and it took a while for her to get back to the table. Congratulations came to her in quiet tones as the next awards were handed out. She politely whispered her thanks and sagged against him. He put his arm around her, offering whatever support he could.

When the awards were over, music played, and people took to the dance floor. Evelyn had another glass of champagne in her hand.

She nodded to their tablemates. "I'm going to make my rounds. I'll be back."

"Don't take too long," her boss said. "We need to talk about what's next."

She took Owen's hand and led him away from the table. "I want to pitch to some other executives while riding this win. Harry wants more of that, and it'll kill me."

"It's okay for you to look for another job with your boss in the room?"

She shrugged. "I don't care. I have an idea for a great show. Harry doesn't want to listen. I'll find someone who will."

He looked at the glass in her hand. "Are you sober enough for that?"

"We're all tipsy. I'll be fine." He stood by and watched her work the room. It was the only way to describe it. He'd been to industry events with her before, and schmoozing was constant in this world. But tonight she was in rare form. She sought people out and was a low-key salesperson. She pitched her idea to people, and they made tentative plans for meetings. While pitching, she managed to be both businesslike and chatty. It put him a little on edge because he didn't like her phoniness, but he accepted that was how business was done. By the time they'd made their circuit back in the direction of the table, Evelyn grabbed another glass of champagne.

"I'm gonna run to the bathroom. You okay to get back to the table alone?"

"I'm not drunk. Just fuzzy enough to numb the disgust I feel at myself for the episode that won me the award I've coveted for years."

He watched as she wove through the crowd, and then he ducked out to the bathroom. He hated coming to these functions with her. So many of the people were fake—their bodies, their personalities, even their manners. He had a hard time reconciling the Evelyn he knew with the woman he saw at things like this. She knew how to play the game, but he wasn't good at navigating it. He was grateful he was nothing more than a visitor to this world.

When he got back to the ballroom, he didn't see her at the table. He sure as hell didn't want to sit and chat with her colleagues, so he walked the perimeter of the room looking for her. He found her on the dance floor in the arms of her ex, and he resisted the urge to pull the man away. She had a right to dance with whomever she wanted, but he didn't have to like it. He came closer, and the look on her face made him think she wasn't a willing participant in the dance. Her eyes were sharp and although he couldn't hear what she was saying, she was not happy. He came up behind Donald and tapped his shoulder. "Can I cut in?"

Donald released his grip on her and turned to face Owen. "You might want to take her home now."

Through clenched teeth, she said, "Fuck you. I do *not* need to be handled."

Ignoring her words, Donald continued to address Owen. "She almost went off on Harry, which would not bode well for her career. I think she's had a bit too much to drink. She never was good at monitoring her alcohol."

She opened her mouth, but Owen spoke first. Everything about this man rubbed him wrong, but all he said was, "You can go now."

Without giving him another thought, he took Evelyn in his arms and continued the dance. He moved them away from Donald and asked, "What the hell was that about? I left you alone for ten minutes."

"I got to the table, and Harry wouldn't shut up about the shooting episode. How great it was. How I pulled so much quality and emotion from everyone. He feels like I found my niche. I might've said something along the lines of how I didn't want my niche to be about parading hurting kids on camera."

He did a mental fist pump, glad she stood up for herself.

"Then Donald stepped in and asked me to dance. Really, he pulled me away. Then you showed up. Just in the nick of time. Like always." She laid her cheek on his shoulder.

"Donald and Harry are both assholes."

"But they're powerful, successful assholes. Donald was being nice by pulling me away before I said something really stupid to Harry. You were there for the rest." She sighed and turned her head so her face was in the crook of his neck.

Her breath fluttered against his pulse point, distracting him. He cleared his throat. "Like I said, asshole."

"I'm glad you came with me tonight."

"I'm glad I could be here for you." He didn't want to think what would've happened if she'd come solo.

The song ended, but she stayed in his arms. Lifting her head, she said, "Take me home."

The words shouldn't have caused any kind of sexual ideas, but they did. He pushed the inappropriate thoughts aside. "Let's go."

EVELYN SLID INTO OWEN'S CAR. WHEN HE GOT BEHIND the wheel, he asked, "Are you okay?"

"I'm fine." She was buzzed but not drunk. She'd known exactly what she was saying to Harry. She just had a hard time mustering a fuck to give. Snippets of the school shooting episode flashed in her mind, making her feel ill all over again. She licked her lips. "As I watched the reel of that episode, I felt sick to my stomach. All I could think was, 'I did that? Who am I?' I didn't used to be like that, okay with putting people's despair on screen."

Owen didn't say anything, but he laid his hand on the seat between them, palm up. She interlocked her fingers with his, and it steadied her.

"I don't care that it was our highest-rated show. I could never do that every week. And Harry wants me to do more like that? Hell no."

"What will happen if you tell him no?"

"I don't know. I have a contract, but I'm sure there's a loophole that will enable them to fire me." Again, at the moment, she didn't care. That was a problem for future Evelyn. She just wanted to put this night behind her.

The glass award sat on her lap. She stroked its smooth edges.

"What's up with Donald? You've been divorced for so long. Why does he keep popping up?"

"We work in the same industry. Our paths are likely to cross at least tangentially. And we're friends."

The fingers of his left hand tightened on the steering wheel, but his right hand remained gentle in hers. "Why are you friends?"

Owen's question scratched at her when she was already irritated. "Why are we friends? Why is anyone friends? Donald and I have known each other for almost fifteen years, five of which we were married. He's not a bad guy."

Owen huffed. She waited for a comment.

"He hurt you. That makes him bad in my book."

She hated that Owen could sweep away her irritation with a couple of short sentences. But that was him. He always had her back. More than anyone else in her life. "Well, not everyone can be as good as you are."

He rolled his eyes, and she laughed.

When they got to her condo, he parked in his spot. She smiled. Owen had a spot in her lot. Of course, it wasn't really his spot, but no one else ever used it.

"You don't have to walk me in. I know you have to get home to Probie and sleep for work."

He didn't respond. He simply got out and walked around to her side of the car, waiting to take her hand as she stepped out. "Are you sure you're okay?"

"Yes," she said, full of attitude that might've been a little more believable if she hadn't wobbled after closing the door.

Owen put an arm around her and guided her to the lobby. Instead of putting up a front and fighting him, she leaned into his warmth and strength.

"Thank you for coming with me tonight."

"You thanked me earlier." They stepped onto the elevator without him letting her go.

"I know you don't like those things, and it doesn't help that you feel the need to swoop in and rescue me."

"I do not."

"You do. It's who you are. But it probably prevents you from having too much fun."

"I always have fun when I'm with you."

"I have fun, too. Plus you look really hot all dressed up."

"You're not so bad yourself."

She fanned herself. "Whew. You better watch it, giving out compliments like that."

"You don't need to fish for compliments. You're sexy and you know it. Every guy in the room stops to look at you. They shoot me jealous glares because I'm lucky enough to have you on my arm."

"Damn, you're good," she mumbled. Her conversations with Nina crashed through all the inappropriate thoughts she'd been having about him. Why did they have to be inappropriate? She suddenly couldn't come up with a single reason why sleeping with her best friend was a bad idea. The elevator dinged and they walked to her door, their bodies brushing with each step, sending warm licks of awareness through her. Owen opened the door and pulled her through.

Evelyn dropped her purse, set her award on the table, and kicked off her heels.

"You need help with anything before I go?"

She grabbed the lapels of his jacket. "Yeah." Then she pressed her lips to his.

For a brief moment, their lips touched, their breath

mingled, and time froze. Evelyn didn't know what she was doing or thinking, but she knew she wanted to stay in his arms. Tilting her head, she opened her mouth and swiped her tongue out.

When her tongue touched his, he let out a groan. Then he firmly planted his hands on her hips and pulled away. He didn't say anything, but his eyes burned into hers. His look said it all. He wanted her as much as she wanted him. Yet he kept her at arm's distance.

She took his hand and tugged. "Come on."

He pulled away, put his hands on her shoulders, and turned her. "Go to bed. I'm going to get you a glass of water and some aspirin."

"I'm not drunk."

"Sure."

She went to her bedroom and waited. When he came in carrying a glass, she turned her back to him and scooped her hair up. "Unzip me?"

He sighed as if she were trying his patience. He set the glass and pills on her bedside table and then unzipped her dress. His fingers brushed her back, and his breath was like a feather against her skin. She wanted to feel his hands everywhere. She tugged at the front of the dress and let it drop.

Stepping from the dress pooled at her feet, she wrapped her arms around his neck. When she leaned in to kiss him again, he stopped her.

"Not like this, Evelyn."

"What are you talking about?"

"You're drunk."

"Tipsy."

"Really buzzed."

"I'm thinking clearly. I want this, and so do you."

"Not when there's room for regret or uncertainty. I can't let you use me to feel better and then pull away again."

What? They'd used each other last time. They'd agreed on that going in. She hadn't pulled away by herself. They both had. "You're the one pulling away now."

"I'm talking about afterward." He stepped back and waved a hand toward her bed. "Get some sleep."

She huffed and crawled into bed, giving him a full view of what he could be having right now. Flopping against the pillows, she said, "You know just as well as I do that we've both been thinking about it a lot lately. I don't know exactly how or when things started to change, but they have. You feel it."

He opened his mouth, but she held up a hand.

"Please do me the favor and don't deny it. Drunk or sober, I'd say this. If you don't want to act on it, I'll accept that, but don't pretend it doesn't exist."

He pressed his lips together and nodded. "Okay."

She swallowed hard. Did he not want to act on it? Had she just blown the best friendship she'd ever had? He backed out of the room.

At the door, he said, "Drink the water. I'll call when I get off work."

She did as he said and gulped the water. It didn't do anything to remove the dusty feeling in her mouth or push past the tightness in her throat as she watched Owen leave.

OWEN SPENT TWO RESTLESS NIGHTS REPLAYING everything Evelyn had said. He hadn't felt this mixed up and confused since he was a teenager. He believed in being honest and up-front with anyone he was involved with. That meant that if he had feelings beyond lust and attraction, he said so.

Except with Evelyn. With her, he'd ignored the lust and attraction. Their emotional attachment to each other had been obvious. They did everything together. They celebrated and commiserated. They turned to each other first for everything important in their lives.

However, the lines had always been a little fuzzy because of the physical attraction. When they'd first met, they had admitted to the attraction and then backed off because they weren't in a place for a relationship. Even as they'd become friends, his attraction to her had never waned. He'd just pretended it wasn't there.

Lately, she'd been making it difficult to discount their chemistry.

What the hell am I supposed to do? He was used to her brand of avoidance, making jokes to keep things light. But when she'd crawled into bed and asked him not to deny their attraction, he hadn't known what to say. It was unlike her to call him out like that. She'd said she would understand if he didn't want to act on it. His body hadn't needed a second to think. It had screamed for him to pounce.

Luckily, he wasn't a clueless teenager anymore. He knew what was at stake. Could they go there and be okay? What was the likelihood it wouldn't work out? They already spent all their time together. They knew each other's quirks and bad habits, and they still liked each other.

Maybe Nina had been right all along.

All day yesterday, he'd been plagued with snippets of conversations and innuendo that Nina had made over many cups of coffee at Sunny's. Of course, it didn't help that it had been the slowest day on earth at the firehouse. They'd cleaned equipment, gone grocery shopping, and played too many hands of poker. He hated shifts like that. They gave him too much time to be in his own head.

He was so bored and desperate for a distraction that he offered to cook breakfast, even though they were off in a little while.

"Hey, knucklechuck," Tony called from the table. "Those pancakes are gonna burn. If I wanted a crap breakfast, I'd wait until I got home to eat."

Owen flipped Tony the bird and then turned the pancakes. So they were a little dark. It wasn't like it mattered. These guys would eat almost anything.

Karen came up behind him and poured herself a cup of coffee. "Where's your head? You've been out of it all shift."

"Got a lot on my mind, that's all."

Jamal clicked the remote to mute the TV. "Sounds like woman problems. What's her name?"

"Don't worry about it." He took the pancakes off the griddle and poured the next batch.

"You know that just piques our interest more," Karen said, hopping up to sit on the counter.

Jamal twisted on the couch to face him, early-morning news no longer holding his attention. "What does Evelyn say about it?"

"Evelyn?" Karen asked.

"His friend." Jamal put air quotes around "friend" as if no one in the room could figure out his meaning from his tone. "Haven't you ever met her? She usually comes to barbecues and stuff."

Karen shook her head. "Is she like your wingwoman or something?"

"Or something," Owen answered. He pulled the last of the pancakes off the griddle and set them on the counter. "Food."

"Come on. Details," Karen prodded.

He didn't respond. He just turned to the sink to clean up.

Karen moved next to him and bumped his shoulder. "All joking aside, if you need to talk..."

"Thanks, but I'm good." It was mostly true. Nothing in his life was falling apart. He didn't need to unburden himself to his coworkers. Though calling his brother Dave might help.

Guys from the next shift started coming in, and he almost regretted having to leave. At least while on shift, he could avoid having to actually do anything.

His phone pinged in his pocket. He pulled it out. Heading to work. Dinner tonight?

Was the woman in his head? She offered him no

escape. He told her to come over after work. That bought him another twelve hours or so to figure shit out. Nothing like being under a deadline. Knowing Evelyn, she would definitely want to talk about what had happened. Or what hadn't happened.

When he got to his car, he called Dave, knowing his brother would already be at work.

"Hey. What's up?"

"Got some time to talk?"

"Sure."

Owen didn't know where to start. He pulled into traffic and headed for home.

"You need to say something for it to be considered talking."

"How did you know that Alicia was the one?"

"I fell in love with her. I couldn't imagine my life without her. What are you getting at?" Maybe Dave wasn't the best person. He'd waited until he was in his thirties to get engaged. He didn't already have a failed marriage under his belt.

"I've been thinking about Evelyn."

"It's about time."

"Why does everyone say that shit?"

"Because even an idiot could see how perfect you guys are together."

"We're best friends. But my track record for relationships isn't great. What if I fuck this up? I'd lose my best friend."

Movement on the line told him that Dave was probably standing so he could pace. His brother was a pacer when he talked.

"I think the bigger question is what happens if you

don't act? Don't you still run the risk of losing her? Evelyn's not going to be alone forever. I'm kind of surprised she's been single this long."

Everything Dave said echoed Nina's words. What was wrong with not wanting change? "I don't want to lose what we have. I want things to stay the same."

"Like the saying goes, the only constant in life is change. You grow, you change. You're not the same person who married Stacy. What happened wasn't your fault."

He knew that. Stacy had chosen to cheat on him with someone she claimed was a friend. But maybe if Owen had paid closer attention, he would've seen what was lacking in their marriage and stopped it from imploding. He'd been clueless, and he'd lost everything.

His inability to see what was right in front of him made him guarded. He swore he'd never be so foolish again. From that point on, he'd protected his heart by not letting anyone get too close. Except for Evelyn. She'd sneaked past every defense he had.

"Do you love Evelyn?"

His gut reaction was to say yes, but he stopped and measured his words. "She's my best friend. I love her. But am I in love with her? I don't think so."

"But you can picture it. If you gave it half a chance, you'd be head over heels ready to walk the aisle again."

"Don't get crazy, man. I'm in no hurry for marriage."

"This is Evelyn we're talking about. You've never trusted anyone like you do her. I think you trust her more than you trust me."

"Well, you did steal my baseball card collection when we were kids."

"Let it go, man."

They laughed, and Owen felt better. He parked in front of his house and said goodbye.

"Before you hang up, keep an open mind. Talk to her. Let her know what worries you."

"I will. Thanks."

"You did remember to request time off for the wedding, right?"

"If I hadn't, it'd be a little late now. It's been set for months, bro. I'll be there. Have my flight booked and everything." What kind of brother would he be if he'd forgotten? The wedding was in less than two weeks.

"I figured, but Alicia has been nagging me to check. Call later if you need to talk more."

"Will do."

He went inside and grabbed Probie's leash. A run always cleared his head.

Chapter Five

For the two days after the award ceremony, Evelyn threw herself into producing the follow-up show. Harry had tried to talk to her twice since then, and she'd successfully dodged him. She couldn't commit to doing more shows like that one. If Harry wouldn't let her do the new show she'd pitched, she'd have to find someone who would.

Everything was in place for the episode she'd planned, B-roll footage, a few well-placed clips from the original episode, and guests who could speak on the volatile subject—none of whom were the kids who had suffered this tragedy. Harry and Trent would get their sparks and excitement, and she could hold on to the shreds of her soul.

In three days, they'd film. Three more days of dodging Harry.

She'd also successfully avoided thinking about Owen. But now the clock was counting down. She knew he needed space to think, so she didn't contact him while he was on duty. But she refused to bury her head. They were good together, and it made sense for them to take it to the next level. They already acted so much like a couple. They turned to each other for comfort and security. They shared everything about their lives. They laughed and cried together. They just fit. If she let him, Owen would hide and pretend she hadn't kissed him or invited him into her bed.

She was done with that shit. She wanted him. Tonight, he needed to make a decision. If he didn't want her, that was fine. She'd get over it. But she was done dancing around each other. Their chemistry was getting hard to ignore. They'd still be friends, but she wanted more. If he couldn't—or wouldn't—give her more, then she'd seek it elsewhere. Just like her job. It was time to go after what she wanted.

She really hoped Owen wanted her as much as she wanted him.

Leaving the studio, she texted to see if he wanted her to grab dinner. Sometimes he liked to cook, but other times, when coming off a shift, he wanted takeout. He quickly responded that he'd ordered Chinese.

No other conversation or question. Just a quick answer.

No way was she going to let him make this weird. When she got to his house, she grabbed her overnight bag from the back seat. Even if she didn't end up spending the night with him, she didn't want to stay in her work clothes.

But she really wanted to spend the night. Not on the couch. Not fully clothed. Taking a deep breath, she walked up the steps and let herself in his house.

Soft jazz played, and a small candle lit the center of his coffee table in the living room. She tried not to get her hopes up. "Hey," he said, coming from the kitchen. He wore his post-run outfit: a pair of low-slung sweatpants and a worn T-shirt.

She looked around. "Where's Probie? He always greets me."

"I think I wore him out on our run. Ready to eat?"

"I'm starved, but I want to change first. With my luck, I'd spill something and it's a bitch to get stains out of this blouse." She knew from experience. She'd spilled coffee on it a couple of times already.

"I'll get the food set up. I was getting ready to put it in the oven because I wasn't sure how long you'd be working." He turned to go back to the kitchen.

She went to the bathroom and changed into the yoga pants and tank top she'd brought, carefully folding her work clothes and tucking them into her bag. She looked at the box of condoms she'd packed, hoping she'd have a use for them. Back in the living room, Owen sat on the couch, containers of Chinese food spread across the table. It was like any other night they'd shared dinner.

Except for that damn candle.

She set her bag next to the couch, and he looked up at her. His gaze traveled over her body as if he had never looked at her before. It was like the charged glances they'd been sharing, only amplified. *That's a good sign, right?*

She sat down beside him. Her nerves got the better of her, so without waiting, she picked up a container and stabbed the chopsticks into it, not caring what it held. Ugh. Sweet-and-sour chicken.

He handed her a plate with fried rice and took the chicken from her, but he didn't start eating. "So," he said.

She scooped up some rice and ate it. "So," she answered around her mouthful.

"I've been thinking."

"Thinking is good. Usually." She forced her voice to remain calm and steady, even though her heart thundered in her chest.

He shot her a look. "I heard you the other day. About us. And the attraction. Yes, I'm attracted to you. I always have been. But changing things between us freaks me out."

"Like I said, things have already changed or at least shifted. I don't know that there's any going back."

"That's what worries me. I date around because it keeps things simple, predictable, like your paternity test episodes. There's no expectation for it to go anywhere with those dates. With you, I'd have expectations."

She put her plate back on the table. "I didn't bring this up because I'm horny. I'm not talking about getting laid." She chuckled. "Well, obviously, that would be part of our relationship. Just not the only part. It would be like us. Only better."

"Owen and Evelyn two-point-o?" he asked.

"Yeah, new and improved."

"What if it doesn't work out?"

She reached over and put her hand on his thigh. He covered her hand with his. The physical reassurance emboldened her.

"How could it not? That's what I've been thinking about. We're good together in every sense. Are you going to suddenly develop some weird habit that'll make me crazy? We know each other better than most. We've seen each other through some rough times. You know I'm always going to be late. I know you need to run in order to think." She waved a hand between them. "This makes sense."

He continued to stare at her, but she couldn't read him. The energy between them took on a life of its own.

"Sex changes things." His voice was rough.

"We both know it'll be good. More than good."

Her nerves took over, so she knew the babbling would start. She'd learned how to control it in professional settings, but in personal interactions, it bubbled up from time to time. Like now, when everything important to her was on the line. "I don't know what else to say or do. I want this, but if you don't, that's okay. I don't fully understand because it's not like I'm asking you to risk more than I am, but I can respect it. I can't deal with the uncertainty—"

His hand came up to her cheek, cradling her jaw. "Shut up, Evelyn."

Then he leaned forward and kissed her, cutting off all words and thoughts. Rationally, she knew this shouldn't feel different. They'd kissed before. Hell, she'd kissed him two nights ago. But the weight of their discussion and the meaning behind the kiss changed everything.

His lips were soft against hers. Slight pressure and gentle nibbling had her leaning toward him, seeking more. His tongue slicked along her lips and into her mouth.

He held her head, his fingers threading into her hair. Her palms rubbed his chest, and she surged up to straddle his lap. Pressing her body tight to his, she wiggled her hips. He moved his hands to her ass and held her close.

He groaned, and the vibration of it moved through her. But they didn't do more. They were enjoying making out and touching each other while fully clothed, getting as hot and horny as teenagers. Lust pooled low in her belly as she felt him harden beneath her. When they came up for air, they stared into each other's eyes.

"So we're doing this?" she asked quietly.

"We're doing this."

She slid off his lap and tugged him to stand.

He let go. "As much as I'd like to get you naked, I'm not leaving this food out for Probie to get into. He'll be shitting all over the floor for days."

Evelyn laughed. "Way to ruin the mood. I thought you had mad skills."

"You're a sure thing," he said with a wink.

She bumped her hip into his and helped him carry food into the kitchen. They haphazardly shoved everything into the fridge, out of the dog's reach.

"We can eat first, you know. We have all night. No curfew," he said.

"Food will be there later. We can work up an appetite." She wrapped her arms around his waist and kissed him again. Then trailed her tongue down the side of his neck. Right now, she was hungry for something other than Chinese takeout.

Owen couldn't think straight. Hell, he couldn't think at all. He was taking Evelyn to bed. Evelyn. His Evelyn. The weight of that pulled at him, but his hard-on couldn't be distracted. He followed her to his bedroom, watching the sway of her hips as she moved. Once across the threshold, she turned and pushed the door shut.

"I love your dog, but I don't want him interrupting," she said quietly. The movement of closing the door put her nearly chest to chest with him.

"Where were we?"

She looped her arms around his neck and tugged. "You were in the process of impressing me with your kissing skills."

"I was, was I?"

"Mmm-hmm." She pressed up and into him, bringing their mouths together.

Molding her to his body, he walked her back to the bed. Before they made contact with the mattress, she yanked at his shirt and the waistband of his pants. He grabbed her hands and stilled them. No way was he going to let her rush him. "We have all night, remember. I'm not in a hurry."

She smirked and slid away. "But Mr. Firefighter, sir, I'm so hot. I'm on fire." She whipped off the shirt she wore and moved onto the bed. Beckoning him with a crooked finger, she continued, "Can you put out the fire?"

The husky breathlessness of her voice made his dick throb. While she leaned back, he snagged the waist of her pants and peeled the soft cotton away from her body. She wore dark blue matching bra and panties. He tugged his shirt over his head and tossed it.

He crawled up her body, placing kisses along her hip, her stomach, the valley between her breasts. He licked his way up her neck to her ear, where he nibbled her lobe before saying, "Just so you know, I have every intention of stoking this fire before I even consider putting it out."

She shivered in his arms, and he wanted more of that. He wanted her to be as completely undone as he was. He reached under her and flicked open her bra. She wiggled out of it as he stroked his fingers back down her torso and past the lacy edge of her underwear. Her eyes fluttered closed.

"Is this okay?" he asked.

She opened her eyes. A furrow wrinkled her brow. "Of course."

He paused, one hand almost inside her panties, the other sliding hair away from her face. "I want this to be good for you. For us. You have to tell me what you want and like."

She let out a low chuckle. "Trust me, if you do something I don't like, I'll let you know. Until then, assume it's all good."

Her words made it all seem so simple.

She shifted, causing his hand to slide farther into her underwear. Her breath hitched as his finger brushed her mound. He slid his hand lower and cupped her. She was warm and wet. His dick pressed against the confines of his underwear and sweatpants.

He stroked her. "I'm not assuming anything, Evelyn. Tell me. Tell me what you want."

She grabbed his wrist and held him against her. "I want you. I want your hands and mouth and dick. I want you to make me come so hard I won't be able to walk. Hard, soft, fast, slow, I want it all." Her palm touched his cheek. "I want everything."

The look on her face was open and honest, a side to her most people rarely got to see. That was his Evelyn. He nodded mutely. His hand stroked her as he lowered his mouth to her gorgeous breast. His tongue circled a stiff nipple while his finger circled her clit. First her breathing sped up, then she began writhing.

He switched breasts and while his mouth worked on one nipple, his free hand played with the other. Evelyn lifted her hips. His palm rubbed her clit, and she gripped his shoulders.

"More," she said.

He rose up so he could watch as she fell apart. He sped up the movements of his hand, moving from sliding fingers inside her to circling her clit, to pressing against it, looking for the magical combination. She lay beneath him, eyes closed, mouth slightly open, skin flushed. Then a moan started deep in her, and her body became taut. Her nails dug into his skin as she trembled and moaned through her orgasm. He held her in his arms until she came down, opened her eyes, and smiled up at him.

That sight alone was enough to get him off for the rest of his life.

"That was amazing," she murmured.

"I hope you don't think that was all I had. I'm just getting started."

"That's good to hear."

Shoving his pants off, he reached over to the drawer and pulled out a condom. While he put it on, she shimmied out of her damp underwear. Her scent filled the air. Blood pounded through his system.

Evelyn pushed herself up to her knees. Lightly touching his shoulders, she caressed the crescent marks her nails had left. Her lips followed the touches, bringing her body in contact with his. Her nipples, still hard, rubbed his chest. For long moments, they knelt there, exploring each other's bodies slowly. Touching, kissing, rubbing, until he couldn't take it anymore.

"I want to be inside you," he said roughly.

"Lie back. Let me take care of you."

He stretched out until his head was on the pillows. Evelyn straddled his prone body and then rubbed against him like a cat until her mouth met his again.

While they kissed, their tongues dancing, she rose up and took him inside her. Languid movements followed, and he became lost in the sensations of her soft body. The wet heat of her mouth and her pussy worked in tandem to drive him blind.

He sat up, keeping her straddling his lap. Their thrusting became shallower, but he was able to hold her. He couldn't believe this was really happening. He was with Evelyn. Naked. Inside her. They were totally clear and sober. He'd dreamed of this so many times over the years. Convinced himself it was an impossibility.

He couldn't imagine anything better. Until she looked into his eyes and smiled. Her entire face was bright, and her smile was one of satisfaction. His chest filled, and it became hard to breathe. If he could freeze time, he would stay right here in her arms with that smile on her face. God, he loved her so much.

Then she shifted so her legs encircled his waist, the movement driving him deeper. Her entire being wrapped around him. Suddenly, he couldn't wait anymore. He flipped so she was on her back again. He buried his face in her neck as he drove into her. Flesh slapping, slick sweat mingling.

He wanted to come, but he wanted her to come again, too, if not with him, before him. "I'm close," he growled.

"So go," she said.

"Are you?"

"I already came."

He lifted to look at her. "Can you again?"

She lifted a shoulder. "Sometimes. Not usually like this. And sometimes I'm too sensitive."

As much as he hated the thought that there was a "usually" that hadn't included him, he wanted to know. He wanted to give her more, be better.

She touched his cheek. "Totally not expected. This is good."

"Let's go for the unexpected." As much as it pained him, he pulled out of her body, immediately missing the heat. He lowered until he shouldered her legs wider and her thighs were at his ears.

She stroked his head. "Owen, you don't have to—"

"Want to," he said against her sensitive flesh.

Her hips bucked in response.

He blew a cool breath against her. "If it's not good, let me know."

Then he used his tongue in light swipes over and around her clit. She didn't tell him to stop, so he continued. It didn't take long until she was panting and gripping the sheet in her fists. When her thighs spasmed against his shoulders, he held tight. As soon as her body sank back to the mattress, he slid inside her once again.

Her muscles squeezed him tight, and it only took a few thrusts for him to see stars. Tingling started at the base of his spine, and his balls contracted. He wanted to hold still and pound deeper all at once. Braced on his elbows, he drove into her again until he was completely empty.

With his muscles twitching, he used his last ounce of energy to slide out of her. He removed the condom and tossed it in the trash before collapsing beside her again. They were both out of breath. She curled against him, and he held her until they were back to normal. When his heart rate and breathing were regulated, his brain fired up.

He just had sex with Evelyn. And they hadn't been drunk, seeking to forget their exes. They'd made the decision to be here. Together.

His heart kicked again. He fisted his hands and reopened them to stop the shakiness. *What the hell have we done?*

"Are you okay?" She stroked his chest.

He patted her hand, surprised that his own was now steady. "Yeah."

"Ready for dinner?"

"I'm not sure I can move."

Sitting up, she asked, "Do you want me to bring you food? You really need to keep up your strength."

And just like that, his panic was gone.

"Funny." Just to prove he could, he pushed up to sit beside her. "Let's go eat."

EVELYN'S PERSONAL LIFE HAD TAKEN SUCH A SHARP TURN that she worried about her professional life. Everything with Owen was damn near perfect. Nothing changed in their friendship, other than the fact that she now had regular non-self-induced orgasms. Why the hell hadn't they done this sooner?

At work, she'd finished taping the school shooting episode. Harry had stopped asking about it, which was almost as worrisome. Instead, he'd switched his focus to sending her ideas that he thought would hit the same emotional notes. No matter how many times she rebuffed him, he came back with more. Like a creepy guy looking to get lucky, he couldn't take a hint. And since he was her boss, she couldn't just tell him no.

The follow-up show was set to air tomorrow. To put it out of her mind, she buried her nose in meetings and phone calls, trying to figure out what else she could bring to the table for Trent. Even the carefree talk show host was growing weary of paternity tests. As she packed her bag for the day with plans to snuggle in bed with a bottle of wine and Netflix because Owen was at work, her phone rang.

She hesitated answering. Few people called her desk. Most used her cell. Except Harry. He always assumed she was at her desk.

"Hello."

"Come to my office. Right now."

"What—"

"Now." Then he hung up.

Shit. So much for her quiet evening.

She slung her bag over her shoulder, intent on leaving as soon as Harry yelled at her for whatever she'd done wrong now.

Knocking on his partially open door, she said, "Hello?"

"Come in," Harry responded sharply.

She pushed the door wide and stepped through. Harry slid his chair back and reclined. He folded his hands over his stomach and pinned her with a look. She waited.

"When we said you should do a follow-up to the school shooting episode, what did we say we wanted?"

Fuck. This was worse than she'd thought. The episode was supposed to air in less than twenty-four hours. She licked her lips and tried to formulate a response.

Harry waved a hand. "Don't. You know what we wanted. We wanted more of the real-person, emotional crap you delivered last year. You had people heated and arguing. Yelling and crying. There was fire," he said, shaking his fist. He shifted and swiveled his computer screen to her. "This is crap."

She stiffened. She'd known he wouldn't be thrilled with what she'd produced, but she did not create crap. "That is a good episode."

"Not what we wanted, though."

"I stand by the work I did."

Harry rose. "It's not enough. We're not airing this as it is. You need to go back and bring in the elements we wanted. We need to see those kids. The audience wants to know where they are, see them being successful in spite of having gone through this."

Tears clawed up the back of Evelyn's throat. "And what about the kids who haven't been successful? Or those who suffer from PTSD? The ones who haven't been able to go back to school? The ones who struggle with survivor's guilt?"

Harry's eyes flared with interest. "Yes, exactly. We want to see the real effects of this."

Her stomach rolled and threatened to pitch her lunch. "They've been through enough. I will not parade them in front of a camera for the world to comment on their misery. It's wrong."

"But it wasn't wrong last year?" Harry asked, his voice rising with irritation.

His dig hit home. "Of course it was wrong. But I was caught up in the moment, in the story. I hated doing it, especially after I saw the final product. We put those kids and teachers through the wringer. We should've protected them. They deserved better."

Harry pressed his lips together, and the muscle in his jaw twitched. "We're pushing the airing. I know you're going out of town this weekend, so you have a week. Fix it or you'll be fired."

This was his line in the sand? "After all our years together?"

"That episode and more like it will put Trent Talks on the map as something more than a fluffy filler. That's what we all want. The bottom line has always been the bottom line."

She pressed her lips together before she said something she'd regret. When Harry didn't continue, she figured she was dismissed. She turned and left his office. Moving like a zombie, she went to her car and drove home. What was she going to do?

Part of her had thought she'd get away with it. She'd taped that show, knowing it wasn't what Harry had demanded, but she thought she'd air it and then go out of town with Owen for his brother's wedding. By the time she returned, Harry would have cooled off and it would be back to business as usual. She should've known better.

As she poured her first glass of wine, her phone rang. Owen. Kicking off her shoes, she answered. "I'm beginning to wonder if you set up security cameras in my house. You always know exactly when I walk in the door."

"I just have excellent timing. How was your day?"

"I don't want to talk about it."

Movement on his end told her that he was moving away from the other guys. The sounds of the TV faded. "What's going on?"

"I just told you I don't want to talk about it."

"I heard, but I also know you'll feel better after you

do. Otherwise, you stew and make yourself more miserable."

Having someone know you that well was both a blessing and a curse. She couldn't get away with a snarky comment. She blew out a heavy breath. "Harry watched the episode."

"And?"

"He hated it. Which shouldn't surprise me. I didn't deliver." Over the last week, as she'd worked her tail off to bring this episode to life, she'd shared her plans with Owen. He'd been impressed with her ideas and take on how to present the sensitive topic.

"What the fuck does that mean?"

"It means that if I don't redo the episode by next week, bringing in the kids and teachers who were there, I'm fired." She choked on the last words. She'd never been fired from a job.

He muttered a curse and paused, the silence pounding against her.

"I don't even know how I can get it done with your brother's wedding this weekend."

"Oh, hell no. You're not canceling this weekend because of your douchebag boss."

She hadn't been thinking about backing out, but Owen's immediate dismissal rankled. "I didn't say I planned to cancel. Which means I have mere days to redo everything." The realization of how little time that was hit her.

"So don't do it."

She wrinkled her whole face as she pulled the phone from her ear. *Did I hear that right?* "What?"

"I said don't do it."

"Did you not hear the part about how I'll be fired if I don't?"

"Not to sound like an asshole, but so what?"

Fear and anger burned across her nerves. How dare he act as though losing her job wouldn't be a big deal? Just walk away from everything she'd worked for? She clenched her jaw, grinding her molars.

"Evelyn."

He said her name so gently, it was like he was standing there, touching her. She began to calm. He had that effect on her, which she usually enjoyed, but right now, it irritated the fuck out of her.

"I know how important your job is to you. I'm just saying that before you decide to kill yourself making Harry happy, think about what it would take to make you happy. You don't enjoy your job anymore. You're looking for something else. Just do it."

Her jaw loosened. She opened her mouth, but before she spoke, his words sank in. What if she walked away? Refused to play into Harry's manipulative game?

"You still there?"

"Yeah," she said quietly, absorbing the possibilities.

"Are you pissed at me?"

"I was…but now, not so much. It's a lot to think about."

"But you'll consider it?"

She inhaled and slowly released the breath. "I don't know. That's huge. To strike out on my own with my pitch and hope someone picks it up."

"I have faith in you. And if you fall on your face and become homeless, I'll let you bunk with me."

Laughter bubbled up in her chest. Leave it to Owen

to piss her off and then cheer her up in the same five-minute conversation. "Thanks, but I have savings. I'm not quite headed to the poorhouse."

"It sounds like you've already made up your mind."

Had she? The thoughts circled her brain, sounding better with each pass. "I'm thinking."

"I'm here if you need to bounce ideas off me."

"I need to take a serious look at my life. And although you're a part of that, this is something I have to figure out for myself."

"Okay. Talk tomorrow?"

"Of course."

They disconnected. She drained her abandoned glass of wine and refilled it. Then she opened her laptop to come up with a plan.

EVELYN SPENT MOST OF THE NIGHT TOSSING AND turning, unsure of what to do. Owen made some valid points, but she hadn't been out of a job since college. She didn't have anything lined up. She had ideas, she had an excellent pitch. Dragging herself out of bed, she dressed and went to the studio, even though no one expected her.

In her office, she looked around. This had been her home for years. Pictures from the show hung on her wall. For so long, she'd thought about where she would place an award. Showcase her ability.

Now she had her award but the guilt she felt about

the show that she won it for ruined it. Owen was right. She was tired of this.

She spun around and took the elevator upstairs. She needed to talk to Harry before she lost her nerve. As the elevator climbed, her heart rate sped up. The doors slid open and she froze. As they started to close again, she stepped out. Rubbing her hands on her thighs, she took a deep breath and marched forward.

Harry's door was open, so she knocked and said, "Got a minute?"

"What are you doing here? You're supposed to be gone this weekend."

"We're leaving later today." She closed the door behind her. "I'm not redoing the episode."

"Evelyn—"

She held up her hand. "I know, Harry. I appreciate everything you've done for me. It's been a great ride, but it's time for me to move on. That episode took a lot out of me, and not in a good way. Not in a it-beat-my-ass-but-I'm-proud-of-the-result way. Those kids, those families, they've been through enough. They deserve to move on without being reminded. I have little doubt that as the anniversary comes they will remember."

"Our job is to share their stories. That's what we do."

"Yes. I don't take issue with that. I have a problem with *how* you want me to do it. The world is shitty enough. I want to spread something to make people feel good."

"You're an excellent producer, Evelyn. Take the weekend. Clear your head."

"I appreciate the offer, but I think we both know that this clearly falls under creative differences. Please have legal draw up the paperwork to end my contract." Her throat tightened as she spoke the words.

"If you're sure..."

"I am." *I think so, anyway*. With a stiff nod, she turned and left the office.

Back in the elevator, her brain ran a loop *of Oh my God. What did I just do?*

But by the time she got out to her car, she her heartbeat was normal, she was breathing calmly, and she wasn't freaked out.

Harry was right. She was a damn good producer. Even if her pitch flopped, she'd be able to get another job. She looked at the time. Twelve hours until her flight for Dave's wedding. So she did was she always did —she'd jump in and give it her all.

OWEN SPENT THE DAY GETTING READY FOR HIS BROTHER'S wedding weekend. He'd tried calling Evelyn when he got off work, but she didn't answer. He didn't like the way they'd left things. He hated seeing the way her job tore her apart.

When they'd first met, she was still new to producing *Trent Talks*. Back then she'd been excited. Over the years, he'd watched that enthusiasm slip away. He'd probably chosen the wrong words yesterday, but he'd meant them. He wished that just once, she'd stand up for herself at work. She was always bending over backward to make things easier for someone else. He didn't get it.

After dropping Probie off at the kennel, he drove to Evelyn's. They had a night flight and had agreed to get a car from her place. When he parked, he was surprised to see her car in its spot. It was only four in the afternoon. She hadn't said anything about leaving work early, although knowing her, she probably still wasn't packed.

He rode the elevator up and used his key to get in. As he closed the door, he called, "Evelyn?"

"Here," she said.

He stepped forward and saw her huddled over her small dining table tucked in the corner between the kitchen and the living room. She didn't look like she'd left all day. He neared her, kissed the top of her head, and said, "Hey."

"Hey," she said without looking up from her laptop.

She reached over, picked up a few sheets of paper, scanned them, held them near her screen, and then put them back down.

"What's going on?"

She blinked rapidly and looked up at him. "I quit."

"What?" He slid the chair out next to her and sat.

"I went to the studio this morning and told Harry that I wouldn't redo the episode. I won't do it to the survivors."

"What did he say?"

"He told me to take the weekend away to think about it."

He waited. Her eyes got big and she smiled. "I told

him I wouldn't change my mind, and that he should draw up the paperwork to end my contract."

Oh shit. He hadn't expected to her jump ship like that. Stand up for herself, yeah, but not just quit.

She laughed. "You look like I should." Taking his hand, she said, "This is good. I haven't felt this relieved in a long time."

"What are you going to do?"

"Well, I have to wait until it's official and I get the actual letter of termination, but I've started making a list of who to pitch to. I've been researching better numbers to use to explain why this is a good show for right now. People need a break from the heavy politics and misery out in the world. They need feel-good. Now I have the numbers to back it up."

He listened and tried to process what she said. But it didn't matter what the words were—she was happy. "You're okay with this decision?"

"I'm not gonna lie. When I first said it, I almost threw up. But the more I thought about it, the easier it got. I'm a good producer. I can make this happen. I just need to find a home for the show."

"They'd be stupid not to hire you."

She leaned forward and kissed him. He briefly wondered when he'd stop being shocked when this happened. Their relationship was the same as always—the casual touches, meaningful conversation—and then they'd kiss and every time, it felt almost like a dream.

When she sat back in her chair, he asked, "Are you packed?"

"Oh my God!" she said with wide eyes.

He shook his head. The woman was always late. "Come on. I'll help."

In the bedroom, he almost tripped over a suitcase.

"Gotcha!" she said and stepped into his space.

"Is that your idea of a joke?"

"Nope. I wanted to lure you into my room so I could have my way with you before we had to go hang out with your family."

He held her hips, pulling her close. "What's wrong with my family?"

"Nothing. Just that, you know…I've known them for a long time and we were just friends. Now things are different. What does that look like? How do we act around them?"

"If you're asking if I'm going to have sex with you in front of my family, the answer is no."

She shoved his shoulder. "You know what I mean. We've been doing this for a couple of weeks, but we haven't told anyone."

"Uh…"

Her eyes narrowed. "What?"

"My brother knows. When I canceled my room, he called me because he thought it was a glitch. I told him I did it. Then he asked if you were supposed to have two double beds instead of the king. When I said no, he got the picture."

Evelyn thunked her head on his shoulder. "If Dave knows, that means your mom knows."

He lowered his mouth and kissed the side of her neck. "If you do the math, that means everyone knows."

"Oh God," she complained.

"Give me a few minutes and I'll have you saying that again in a totally different tone."

"I'm being serious. This is gonna be weird."

"Why?" he asked, continuing to kiss her ear, her neck, her shoulder.

"They'll look at me differently. They'll know we had sex."

That pulled him out of the moment as he laughed. "So what? I know my parents have sex. I just don't think about it. I promise, no one is thinking about us getting it on. Except me." He pulled her toward the bed. "I think we have an hour since we don't have to get your bag packed."

"I don't take that long to get ready."

He laughed again as they fell onto the bed. "Next time, I'll set a stopwatch."

She slipped her hand into his jeans and stroked him, and he forgot everything he was going to say.

Chapter Six

Evelyn had been around Owen's family plenty over the years. Birthday parties, backyard barbecues, weddings. She'd been his date often. Probably a little too often, given the previous status of their relationship. Everyone had always considered them a couple, and they'd just shaken their heads.

After years of convincing everyone they were just friends, they were now a couple. She didn't want to explain to people the how, when, and why of it. Would they ask? Or would they just see them and accept it?

Owen's hand slipped into hers as they walked to the rental car. "You're overthinking this. My family already loves you."

"That's when was I was your friend."

"You're still my best friend. That hasn't changed."

Even though her heart swelled at his acknowledgment, she said, "You keep telling yourself that. Your mom is going to want to interrogate me. That's what families like yours do."

He opened the passenger door for her and put their bags in the trunk. Then he got behind the wheel. "What do you mean, families like mine?"

"You're like a TV sitcom family. You're all friends and you like one another. If you had a sister, I bet anything that your dad would want to sit down with her date and vet him. So it doesn't matter that they've known me for years. Things are different, and they're going to treat me differently." In truth, she had no idea what to expect. Growing up, it had been her and her mother. She pretty much had done whatever she wanted. She'd been on her own.

"We'll see." He interlocked her fingers with his, raised their hands, and kissed hers. "Try not to panic. You can hold your own with anyone from my family."

He drove them to the hotel, and Evelyn gave herself a silent pep talk. He was right. She'd known his family for a long time. They'd always treated her like one of them. Maybe this wouldn't be too bad. She liked the concept of belonging.

When they got to the hotel, Owen grabbed their bags, and she went to check them in. He followed and asked, "Do you want to hide out in the room or go find my family?"

Evelyn signed for the room and looked down at herself.

He sighed. "You look fine."

"You always say that, but it doesn't make it true." She accepted the cards from the clerk. "Would you hate me if I said I'd rather wait until tomorrow?"

"I could never hate you."

The look in his eyes made her believe every syllable. "You can go hang out with your brother or whatever. You don't need to babysit me."

"Crawling into bed with you and relaxing sounds like a great way to spend the rest of my night."

He led the way to the elevators, hefting both of their bags. When the elevator arrived, the doors swished open, and Owen's mom stepped out. Her face brightened and she spread her arms wide. "You're here!"

She rushed forward and threw her arms around him. Because his hands were occupied with luggage, it was a one-sided hug.

Other people pushed around them and got on the elevator. The doors swooshed shut, taking Evelyn's escape with them.

After releasing Owen, Carol turned to Evelyn. She wrapped her in the same kind of hug she'd given her son. "I'm so glad you came."

Evelyn returned the embrace. When Carol stepped back she pointed between Evelyn and Owen. "So this is real, right? David wasn't pulling my leg?"

Owen sighed and rolled his eyes. "No joke. Evelyn and I are a couple."

The woman clapped like a giddy cheerleader. "It's about time." She grabbed Evelyn's hand. "I've been telling Owen for years that you were perfect for him. He's so slow to move, you know? Always has to make sure that he's looked at everything from every angle before committing."

Evelyn sneaked a look at Owen from the corner of her eye. "I'm glad all my angles are approved."

Looping her arm through Evelyn's, Carol said, "Go put your bags in your room and meet us in the bar. Everyone is there."

Evelyn wasn't ready to face the whole family, but now she was feeling cornered.

"Actually, Mom, we were headed upstairs for the night. I was on duty yesterday and Evelyn has a lot going on at work. We're gonna turn in."

"Bah," she said, waving a hand. "You're half my age and I'm still up."

Evelyn patted her hand. "I appreciate the offer, but I'm really beat." She looked to Owen for help. She didn't know what else to say to convince Carol to let her go.

Suddenly her arm was free. With a chuckle, Carol said, "I get it now. Tired. Sure. You could've just said you were going to your room to boink."

Boink? Evelyn swallowed a giggle.

Owen rolled his eyes again. "Thanks, Mom."

She went on tiptoe and kissed Owen's cheek. "I'm old, not dead. Have a good night."

As Carol walked toward the bar, Owen jabbed at the elevator button. He stood stock-still, and Evelyn made it about a minute before she lost it and fell into a fit of laughter.

"Not funny."

"Sure it is. Who the hell uses the word 'boink'?"

"Apparently, my mother."

The doors opened and they stepped in, Evelyn still laughing. "And I was worried about being scrutinized. Had I known that having sex with you would lead to your mother making you uncomfortable, I would've done it a long time ago."

"Watch it. The bar isn't open all night. I can invite them all back to our room." The thought sobered her quickly, but she liked the sound of *our room*. Maybe this wouldn't be as stressful as she thought.

As soon as they made it upstairs, his phone lit up with texts. His brother wanted him to come down for a drink. He declined, even though Evelyn told him to go.

She tried to convince him to enjoy the time with his family. "I'm really just going to shower and get in bed. I want to do some more research while I have the downtime. There's a networking thing next week that I want to score an invite to. I have to figure out who can get me in."

"You think I'm going to have a beer with Dave instead of taking a shower with you? You don't know me at all."

"I didn't invite you into my shower."

"You owe me."

"Owe you for what?" she asked, pulling her shirt over her head, walking backward into the bathroom.

His eyes widened, and he continued to stalk toward her. "For getting you off the hook with my mom. I suffered humiliation for you."

"Hmm...I don't know if that's enough to share my hot water." Down went her pants. She kicked them to the side. The cold tile of the floor battled the heat of her skin caused by his stare.

"I can definitely make it worth your while."

Lust fluttered low in her belly. Then he did the one-handed T-shirt yank that only guys did. *Does he know how sexy that is? Or is he simply being efficient?* Her mouth watered at the movement, watching his abs bunch and flatten.

"Hey, babe. My eyes are up here." He moved his fingers from his chest to his face.

"You're one to talk. You were totally staring at my boobs a couple of minutes ago."

"Got me." He moved forward again, closing in on her, trapping her between him and the sink.

As he pressed his body against hers, she felt his hard-on prodding her. He kissed her, his lips coaxing hers open. He reached around her and flicked her bra clasp. Without leaving her mouth, he slid her bra away and then held her close. Her nipples hardened as they rubbed against the hair on his chest.

She pulled back a couple of inches and whispered, "You're interrupting my shower."

"I'm making sure you need a shower." He lowered his mouth to her neck. His hand moved from her hip down the front of her panties and he stroked her.

She gripped his shoulders. "Keep that up and I won't have the strength to stand up in the shower."

He leaned over and started the water. While it warmed, he continued to play with her body. "Then I'll hold you up."

She had no doubt he would.

EARLY THE NEXT MORNING, OWEN SLIPPED OUT OF BED quietly so he wouldn't wake Evelyn. She never did get back to her research, but they'd been up pretty late. He wanted to get a run in before his family took every minute of his time for the rest of the weekend. He took his clothes and running shoes into the bathroom to get ready.

When he left the room, Evelyn was still sprawled on the bed, hair spread wildly across the pillows. Pulling the door shut behind him, he tried to put the image out of his head or he wouldn't be able to run. He spent a few minutes stretching out in the parking lot of the hotel and then started off at a slow jog. He normally used this time to clear his head, but for the first time in a while, he was happy with his life.

The sun was out, and the temperature was on its way up to blistering, but Owen enjoyed the sights as he ran. The streets were filled with tourists getting ready for a day of sightseeing and gambling. He missed the relative quiet of his residential neighborhood. At home, he occasionally passed a dog walker or another jogger. Within a couple of blocks here, he was dodging people left and right.

He only ran a mile and gave up. As he headed back to the hotel, his phone bleeped. A text from Evelyn asking where he was. Shit. He should've left her a note. He texted her that he was out for a run and would be back soon. Then he reminded her that they had breakfast with the family.

She sent him a string of emojis that he didn't have time to decipher. He picked up his pace and managed to at least work up a decent sweat. Back at the hotel, he walked into the room but didn't see Evelyn. The bed was still a mess, but no sign of her. "Evelyn?"

No answer. He stripped and tossed his clothes in the corner of the bathroom to deal with later. He jumped in the shower and cleaned up. As he shampooed, a knock sounded on the bathroom door.

"Hey, I got coffee."

He stuck his head past the curtain. "There's a maker on the counter."

Her face scrunched. "Ew. I need my morning coffee, but I'm not that desperate."

Sliding back under the water to rinse, he said, "You're a coffee snob."

"Yep. And don't you forget it. Plying me with crappy coffee will get you nowhere."

He opened his eyes and caught her peeking through the door. "Did you want to come in?" he asked with a grin.

"I'm already dressed for breakfast."

He took in what she was wearing. A black skirt, silky-looking purple top, and sexy-as-fuck heels.

"Don't look at me like that."

"Like what?"

"Like you want to strip me."

"You're the one staring at me in the shower."

"I'm enjoying the view."

"So was I." He twisted the knob to turn off the water. He pushed the door open and stepped out.

She handed him a towel. "I'll wait outside."

"Don't trust yourself?"

"Yeah, that's it," she said with a chuckle.

He wrapped a towel around his waist and grabbed the coffee she left on the counter. In the room, he looked around for his bag. "Where are my clothes?"

She gave him a look like maybe he was a little dumb. "In the closet."

"Why?"

"Because that's where clothes go."

He crossed to the closet, took a gulp of coffee, and said, "We're only here for the weekend. What's the point of unpacking?"

"Such a guy. If you don't hang your clothes up, they'll be all wrinkled."

Reaching in the closet, he snagged a shirt and pants. Tossing them on the bed, he put a hand over his heart. "Oh, no. What would I do if I was wrinkled?"

She rolled her eyes. "This isn't a barbecue with your firefighter buddies. This is your brother's wedding." She glanced at the bedside clock. "You need to hurry. We'll be late."

Her warning made him laugh.

"What's funny?"

"You're always late," he said as he dressed.

"But this is a family thing. I want to make a good impression."

"I told you, my family already loves you. You'd have to actively try to make them dislike you."

"It's still weird."

"What?" He ran his hand over his head to make sure his hair was lying flat.

"The whole couple thing in front of your family. Like what are we supposed to do? Tell everyone that we're a couple now?"

He walked to her and took her hand. "I was thinking more along the lines of making out at the table so everyone gets the hint at the same time."

She looked at him with uncertainty in her eyes. "Aren't you nervous at all?"

"Nope. Like my mother said, I don't do things unless I'm sure. I've always been sure about you." He kissed her, and she softened against him.

"Ready?" he whispered against her lips.

"Tricky."

He raised his brows.

"You say all these mushy words and kiss me to make me forget."

"We'll be fine." They finished their coffee just as his phone buzzed with a text. "I'm sure that's my family wondering where we are."

Down in the lobby, his whole family was waiting. "Evelyn takes forever to get ready."

Her mouth dropped open, and she smacked his arm. He grinned and told the truth. Dave walked over and hugged Evelyn. Then he shook Owen's hand. With a nod toward Evelyn, his brother said, "Don't screw this up."

"I have no intention of doing that."

They joined the crowd and got directions for the restaurant they were going to. When they got to the car, Owen asked, "You okay?"

Evelyn smiled brightly. "You were right. I had nothing to worry about. Your family is great."

"Yeah, they are."

THE DAY WHIZZED BY IN A FLURRY OF ACTIVITY. EVELYN had thought she'd be able to sneak away and get some work done, but Owen's family included her in everything they had going on. While the guys went to pick up their tuxes, the women had a spa day.

In between getting facials and manicures, Evelyn had a chance to get to know Alicia, Dave's fiancée. She was a lawyer for a nonprofit with flawless skin and a wicked sense of humor. No wonder Dave had fallen for her. By the time they were polished and pretty, Alicia and her three bridesmaids had convinced Evelyn to join them for the bachelorette party. She pulled out her phone to text Owen while they teased her.

Her phone rang as she opened the messaging app. "I was just about to text you."

"How are things going?"

"Great. Alicia and her friends are a lot of fun."

He released a heavy breath. "Good." He paused. "Dave's got plans for a bachelor party thing that I didn't know about."

"So does Alicia."

"Do you want me to bail on him?"

"What? No." She practically yelled at him. "You should hang out with your brother. Alicia invited me to go out with them."

"Oh."

"That's why I was going to text you. I'm going to go have a few drinks with them."

"Okay. Have fun."

"You, too." She paused and then added, "No hookers."

"Why the hell would I want a hooker when I have you in my bed?"

"Good point. See you later." She disconnected, and Alicia and her friends were staring at her. "What?"

Jenny's brow furrowed. "Are you sure you just started dating Owen?"

"Uh..."

Alicia stepped forward and looped her arms into Jenny's and hers. "I told you, Evelyn and Owen just started dating, but they've been a couple forever. Longer than I've known Dave."

"We've been friends," Evelyn clarified as they stepped out of the spa.

Virginia came up on the other side of Evelyn. "Oh! You fell in love with your best friend."

"I didn't—"

Beth, on the other side of Jenny, said, "That's so romantic. How did it happen? Did he look into your eyes one day and you just knew?"

They all talked so fast that Evelyn didn't know who to answer or what to say. "I—"

Alicia laughed as she nodded toward a limo waiting at the curb. "Knowing Owen, he made a pro/con list before making a move."

Evelyn laughed because it did sound like something he would do. They climbed into the car. "Our relationship just kind of evolved."

Virginia gave the driver the name of the bar they were going to. When she sat back, she patted Evelyn's leg. "I'm so glad you joined us. I'm the only married one here, so I always feel weird when they're all hitting on men."

Beth scoffed. "We do not always hit on men."

"Yeah, we do," Jenny admitted.

"Anyway, it'll be nice to have someone to talk to when they go off to find someone to make out with."

"You guys didn't bring dates to the wedding?" Evelyn asked.

Beth and Jenny smiled. "Of course not. We plan to play the role of sad bridesmaid. Everyone knows that a wedding is the best place to get lucky."

Alicia said, "So glad I could help with your love life."

Before long, they stopped in front of a bar, and the women piled out. Virginia informed her that they had the driver for the night, so if she wanted to drink, they had a safe ride back to the hotel. Evelyn couldn't remember the last time she had a real girls' night out, so she wanted to have a good time.

Four bars and six hours later, Evelyn was feeling pretty happy. While she hadn't indulged in nearly as much alcohol as the bridesmaids, she'd drunk enough to feel fuzzy-headed. She knew she wasn't thinking straight when she couldn't manage to text Owen. After three tries, she gave up and decided she would just see him at the hotel.

She helped Virginia get Alicia tucked in while Jenny and Beth stumbled to their room. Over the course of the night, Evelyn realized that Virginia played mother hen to them all. As they closed Alicia's door, Evelyn said, "You're a good friend. They're lucky to have you."

Virginia waved her off. "I didn't do anything they wouldn't do for me."

Evelyn wasn't sure about that. She waved good night to Virginia and headed to her room. She slid the key card in twice and it wouldn't work. Just as she was about to go to the front desk to get it fixed, the door swung open, and Owen stood wearing nothing but his boxer briefs and a grumpy look on his face.

"Hey," she said. "You're back early."

"They wanted to gamble. I hung out for a while with my brother, but gambling's not my thing."

No, it wouldn't be, she thought. He didn't like to take chances.

He stepped back from the door to let her in. "Did you have fun?"

"Yeah, I did. Alicia and her friends were great."

"Are they all as drunk as you?"

"I'm not drunk. Buzzed. And except for Virginia, they are all far worse off than I am."

"Tomorrow morning is going to be rough for them."

Evelyn tossed her purse on the dresser and began to peel off her clothes as she neared the bed. "I'm glad you're here."

"So am I," he said, watching her move.

"Besides that." She flounced on the messy bed and sprawled out. Staring at the ceiling, waiting for the slight spin to recede, she said, "I love your family."

He climbed into bed next to her. "They're pretty fond of you, too."

She rolled to her side, and he reached out to move her hair and toy with it. She could just spend time looking at him like this—relaxed and…happy? A sense of peace washed over her, but part of her worried that it was manufactured.

"What's on your mind?"

"It's just that, I was thinking about us while the girls were scoping out available guys."

"Alicia and her friends were scoping out guys?"

"Just Jenny and Beth. Anyway, I was thinking this is almost too easy. We haven't had to work for it."

"That's your big complaint?"

"We're taught that we have to work for the good things in life. Without effort, it's easy to lose things. Or let them go." Hell, her voice cracked on the last part. She hated when alcohol made her emotional.

"I'm not letting you go anywhere." He slid an arm under her head and the other around her hip and pulled her close until her face rested on his chest.

She closed her eyes and tried to focus. She didn't think he was leaving, but she couldn't quite verbalize what she did mean. Instead of worrying about it, she breathed in his scent and let it comfort her to sleep.

OWEN WAS HAPPY FOR HIS BROTHER, HE REALLY WAS, BUT he couldn't wait for the wedding to be over. Between the bachelor party and then the rehearsal, he felt out of sorts. He missed his routine. Now he had to go take pictures, but Evelyn wasn't ready.

"Go on without me. I don't need to be there for at least another hour."

But she was always late. He didn't want to have to deal with the comments and questions about his marital status without her on his arm. Unless that was why she was procrastinating. "Do you not want to tell people about us?"

"What?" She poked her face out of the bathroom, makeup artfully done on one eye.

"Do you want to skip telling people about us being together?"

"Of course not. I mean, I don't think we need to make an announcement or anything, but I don't plan on keeping my hands off you like I have at every other family event over the years."

"Sure?"

"Positive. Plus, if people don't realize we're a couple, you're going to have a bunch of single women hitting on you as a sure thing."

He huffed. "Who said I'm a sure thing?"

She arched a brow, which looked silly with one eye made up dramatically and the other plain.

"For you, of course, I'm a sure thing. But if I didn't have you, I might play hard to get."

"I don't believe that for a minute. Go on so you're not late. I know how uptight that makes you. I'll be there before the bride walks down the aisle."

He must've looked unsure because she added, "I promise."

With a quick nod, he left to find his brother and their parents. Alicia wanted to have some photos taken before the ceremony. When he got to the lobby, they were waiting for him.

Dave asked, "Where's Evelyn?"

"She said she'll be down before Alicia walks the aisle."

"Oh. We wanted her to be in the family picture."

Owen froze. Sure, he thought of Evelyn as family, but he hadn't considered whether she should be in wedding pictures.

His mom waved a hand. "We can get another one later. Come on, my handsome boys." She looped her arm through each of theirs, leaving their dad to trail behind.

An hour later, he stood at the front of the chapel with his brother, who didn't seem nervous at all. Owen kept an eye on the door, looking for Evelyn. Then suddenly, she was there, sweeping down the aisle with a bright smile on her face.

Their eyes met, and she winked at him. His mom waved her over to sit with them. The tension in his shoulders eased. He didn't know why he was worried. Evelyn had never lied to him. She said she'd be here, and she was. Dave leaned over and whispered, "You're one lucky man."

"I know," he answered, not taking his eyes off Evelyn. The bridal march started, and he glanced at his brother. "So are you."

Dave slapped him on his back. "Let's do this."

The ceremony was short and sweet. They all moved down the hall to the banquet room for dinner and dancing. As soon as they were through the door, Owen searched for Evelyn again. As she neared, a thought flashed that he wanted her all the time. This was a forever thing.

When she'd asked if he ever wanted to remarry, the thought hadn't occurred to him. But seeing her here, now, during his brother's wedding, had him reevaluating. Like Evelyn had said, there was something about having someone to come home to. As soon as she was within touching distance, he reached out and pulled her in for a kiss.

He wouldn't tell her what he'd been thinking, but he let his kiss hint at it. They had time to address things. A moment later, he was being nudged. Hard.

He looked up, where Alicia stood holding champagne and Dave's elbow was ready to connect with his side again.

"We're supposed to be the only ones sucking face today," Dave said.

Evelyn blushed and looked around. A few people had taken notice of them kissing, like his cousin Maria, which meant that anyone who didn't know that he and Evelyn were a couple would know within the hour.

Alicia handed them both a glass.

Evelyn raised hers and said, "To the bride and groom. May you have a happy, healthy marriage."

They clinked glasses, and then Dave said, "Mom wants more pictures."

Owen groaned.

Evelyn bumped him with her hip. "Don't be a baby. It's not every day that she gets to see her son get married."

"At least for me, this'll be the only time," said Dave.

Owen shot a dirty look at his brother.

Dave raised his hands, one still holding his champagne. "It's not my fault you were careless in your choices when you were young."

Being roasted was not helping.

Evelyn, however, laughed. "You're supposed to make mistakes when you're young. That's how you learn." She stroked his jaw. "Besides, I like this older, wiser version of Owen."

He couldn't help it. His chest puffed out with pride. Evelyn always knew what to say to keep everyone happy.

Mom joined them. "Good. You're all in one place. I swear herding you as adults is a hundred times worse than when you were kids. Let's go before the photographer moves."

"Have fun," Evelyn whispered, and drank from her glass.

"You, too," Mom said to Evelyn. "You missed all the pictures at the ceremony. I want a nice family photo."

"Uh..."

She looked to Owen for help, but he said nothing. If he had his way, she'd be in all his pictures. He took her empty glass and set it on a table. Slipping his hand in hers, he led her behind his mom and Dave. Evelyn tugged his sleeve.

"What are you doing?"

"Apparently, taking more pictures."

"You know what I mean."

"Since when are you camera-shy?"

She pulled him to a stop. "What kind of message is this sending your mom and your entire family?"

"It was my mom's idea, but I don't have a problem with it. They love you. I love you." He'd told her he loved her before. The words weren't new, but the look on her face was. To ease whatever thoughts were racing through her head, he added, "It's just a picture."

She didn't argue or try to pull away. He wasn't used to seeing Evelyn unsure of anything. She was a woman who always knew what she wanted and went for it. For her to be unsure of her place in his life unsettled him. Slipping an arm around her waist, he whispered in her ear, "There's no one I would rather have in a family photo."

"It feels so official. Taking a family photo at a wedding."

He chuckled. "Afraid people are going to start hounding you about when you'll be next?"

"Kind of. Aren't you? This is your family. They'll hound you before they come after me."

"Won't bother me a bit. I've been dodging them and their questions for years. When it happens, it happens."

"When, huh?"

"I think you're a safe bet."

"I thought you didn't like to gamble."

"I don't, unless I know how the hand will play out." They joined the rest of his family, and he turned Evelyn so she was in his arms in front of the camera. Their relationship didn't feel like a gamble at all. It felt right.

EVELYN HAD A GREAT TIME AT THE WEDDING. ALL OF HER fears about things being different were unfounded. The wedding was small, and almost all of the family in attendance were people she'd met numerous times over the years. No one commented on her relationship with Owen. Then her phone started blowing up with texts.

Nina: Oh my God. What is going on?

Tess: When did this happen?

Even Trevor sent her one:

About time

She stared at the screen. Then she looked up to where Owen was on his way back from the bar.

"You couldn't just leave the phone for one night?" he asked as he neared.

"Of course I can. In fact, until it started vibrating like crazy, I didn't pull it out." She turned the phone to show him. "Want to tell me what this is about?"

He set their drinks on the table and glanced at the phone. It took a second, but then acknowledgment lit his eyes. "Probably the picture I posted to Facebook."

"What picture?"

"My mom took one of us dancing."

She looked at him, because a dance wouldn't cause this kind of stir.

"And kissing."

"Don't you think that's something you should've run past me first?"

He sat beside her and took a pull from his bottle of beer. "You said you weren't looking to keep us a secret. It's a good picture."

"But these are our friends. We should've told them together."

He leaned over, putting one arm on the back of her chair. "Look. We're in a relationship. I'm pretty fucking happy about that. I don't care who knows. That picture told the world, and I didn't have to say a word."

She smiled. "So this was just about being efficient."

"This was about letting everyone know that in addition to you being my best friend, we're now a couple. No doubt. No confusion. No question."

Something about the surety with which he spoke caused her heart rate to spike. She hadn't known how much she needed that reassurance. She liked being in their own little bubble, but it had been a couple of weeks, and she hadn't told anyone. It was like by not saying something she was hiding their relationship. But deep down, she had a pang of uncertainty, fear that he would back away.

"Okay," she said quietly. Picking her phone back up, she found the picture and reposted it. If Owen could take the leap and let the world know about them, so could she.

While she tapped away on her phone, Owen trailed his hand from her knee up her thigh, just shy of sliding up her dress. He leaned to her ear and said, "Think they'd notice if we left?"

"You're the best man. It's a small wedding. Everyone will notice."

Her phone vibrated on the table. She picked it up with the intention of putting it back in her purse, but it was Donald. As far as she knew, he wasn't a friend on social media. At least not on her personal profile.

Owen glanced down at the screen and groaned as he sat back. "That dude is the biggest cockblock I've ever met."

Evelyn slid her hand up his thigh and squeezed. She

brushed her lips against his ear. "No one is going to block me. While I take this call, why don't you figure out a way to get us out of here without ticking people off?"

His breath hitched, and he pressed his hand on top of hers. If she didn't move soon, things were going to get indecent. She gave him a quick kiss on the lips and pulled away. "I'll be back in a few minutes."

She walked out of the small banquet room to find somewhere quiet to talk. As she dialed Donald's number, she sat on a plush bench in a side hall. "Hello, Donald."

"Is it true?"

"I'll need a little more than that to go on. Is what true?"

"You quit Trent Talks?"

"Not exactly. Harry refused the version of the school shooting episode I prepared. He told me to redo it or I'd be fired. I refused."

"Evie, why would you do that? Trent is on the rise. He's going places."

"I don't need to follow Trent. I'm good at what I do."

"I wasn't implying you're not. But people talk. If they think you're difficult to work with, they won't hire you."

"I'm difficult for standing my ground against something that's wrong? If you did this, they'd cheer you on for being so ethical."

"I don't make the rules, Evie."

The nickname made her cringe in a way it never had before. "I'm at a wedding right now, so if that's all…"

"I saw the picture of you and Owen. I had a feeling that was going to happen sooner or later."

"You did?"

"He's been a stabilizing force in your life. Something lights up in you when you talk about him. Does he make you happy?"

"Yes," she said freely.

"Then I'm happy for you. The other reason I called was because I want you to send me your pitch."

"What pitch?"

"The new talk show. Did you think I forgot? I'm considering moving back to Chicago. I have a line on some prospects. You know that city better than most."

She was torn. Donald always had connections. He'd gotten her a head start in this business, but she'd been doing well on her own for a long time now. She took a minute and then agreed. It would be silly to cut off a possible opportunity simply because it came from her ex.

"Talk to you later."

For a minute after disconnecting, she sat in silence. A shadow near her caught her attention. Owen had come to find her.

"Everything okay?"

"Yeah. Donald heard I'd quit."

"Why would he care?"

She stood and tucked her phone in her purse. "I told you before, we're friends. But he also asked me to send him the pitch for my new show."

"Why?"

"He's thinking about moving back to Chicago."

He narrowed his eyes but said nothing. "I'm really glad I'm not a mind reader because your head is probably a scary place right now."

"I don't like him."

"I know, but he's always helped with my career. While I haven't needed to ask him for any favors recently, he's been there. I don't want to turn to him now, but I have to find someone willing to take a chance on me."

"You'll find someone else. You have that networking thing next week, right?"

"Yep. You'll be my plus-one?"

"Of course. Now let's get out of here before anyone notices."

Chapter Seven

After the weekend of festivities, Owen and Evelyn flew back home late Sunday night. He had to be on shift Monday morning, so Evelyn said she'd get Probie from the kennel. She'd skipped coffee with the New Beginnings crew because she was exhausted. Nina and Tess sent a couple of texts teasing her for avoiding them, but she promised details soon.

Her morning at the studio had been pretty much what she'd expected. Harry already had her resignation papers drawn up. They were sitting on her desk when she got there with an empty box to pack her things. She'd thought it would be more stressful, but she felt eerily fine.

She had her desk cleared—except for the paperwork waiting for her signature—and moved onto the bookcase when Tanya knocked on her open door.

"Is it true?" She looked at Evelyn and didn't wait for a response. "Did he fire you?"

Evelyn smiled. "I resigned. Creative differences."

"Bullshit. What really happened?"

"Harry wanted me to redo the school shooting anniversary episode."

"What we put together is awesome. We've gotten excellent feedback. He's seen the numbers, hasn't he?" She leaned against the arm of the battered couch.

"Doesn't matter. He issued the ultimatum last week. I quit. I had already pitched a new show to him and told him that you and Luke could handle Trent Talks. I'm ready to move on."

"Fuck. I'm gonna miss working with you. Luke is a stick in the mud who gets uptight every time I swear. He might as well be clutching his pearls."

Evelyn chuckled. "He's not that bad."

Tanya rolled her eyes. "Maybe not, but he's not you."

Evelyn packed the books that she wanted to keep from the shelf. Most were just dust collectors that she decided to leave. "You might want to lobby to get my office before Luke does."

"Really?"

"Why not? You have the same amount of experience as he does. There's no reason you can't run it. I'd be happy to put in a good word with Harry, but I don't think he's too happy with me right now."

"Thanks. Maybe I'll head upstairs now."

"Go for it."

Tanya moved away from the couch. "Where are you going next? Any ideas?"

"I'm pitching to a number of people. I'd love to get this new show picked up, but if not, I'll send my resume around."

"I'm sure you won't be sitting for long. I don't think Harry realizes what he's losing."

Evelyn scrunched her nose. "I don't think he cares."

Tanya reached out and gave her a hug. "Let me know where you land. And if you need an assistant, I'd follow you in a heartbeat."

"I'll keep that in mind." They let go and Evelyn added, "Don't let Luke or Trent push you around. You know what works. Make them follow you."

"Thanks for everything." Tanya left and Evelyn looked around.

Yeah, she was ready to be done here.

Evelyn spent the next two days talking with Marilyn about the show and developing a list of ideas.

The more she had prepared, the more attractive the show would be. Evelyn hesitated sending the pitch to Donald. If she worked with him, it might make Owen a little crazy; he really hated her ex. Although Donald hadn't been a very good husband, he'd always been an excellent producer. He created magic with every idea he gave the green light to. It didn't mean she necessarily wanted to work with him. Part of her worried about him taking control of everything. And this was her baby, not his. Donald would never be like Owen. He couldn't step back and let her do her thing.

She'd been spending every night at Owen's house, but tonight, she was at her place to get ready for the networking event. Owen said he'd pick her up as soon as he got off his overtime shift, assuming, of course, no calls came in. He'd been grabbing a few extra shifts when asked. Normally it didn't bother her. Tonight she prayed for a quiet evening. She really wanted him at her side.

At eight-thirty, he was calling from the door to let her know he was there. She slid into her pumps and walked into the living room.

"Wow," he said.

"I'm sure you've seen me wear this before," she said, looking down at her outfit. It was her favorite little black dress.

"Probably. But I could never do this before." He pulled her into his arms and kissed her. He wrapped one hand around her nape, and the other cupped her ass, bringing her flush against him.

When he broke the kiss, she realized that she had a tight grip on the lapel of his jacket. She smoothed it out. "I think wow is an understatement."

"You saw me in this suit for Tess's engagement."

"I was talking about the kiss."

"I can do better than that."

"I bet you can, but we have to go. We'll be fashionably late enough that all the people I want to talk to should be there and well-lubricated with alcohol, but not so drunk they don't remember our conversation."

He shook his head. "Always scheming."

"Not scheming. Finessing."

His face said he wasn't buying any of it, but he wasn't part of this industry. In his world, he took people as he saw them. People in TV had their own special dance of schmoozing. You never knew when you'd need a favor from someone, so there was always a fine veneer on every interaction. It was nowhere near as black-and-white as Owen would like it to be.

"So how does this work?" he asked as they parked near the hotel where the event was taking place.

"We get a drink and mingle. Chat up the executive producers. See what they're in the market for. Gather business cards."

"Which means what for me?"

"Stand there and look sexy."

He bent his elbow for her to take. "I think I can handle that."

Wrapping her arm around his, she patted him. "I don't need you to do anything but be here for me. Moral support."

"I can definitely accommodate you."

All of the ideas racing through her mind settled as he looked into her eyes. A stabilizing force. That's what Donald had called him. In that moment, she understood what he'd meant.

"You got this." He gave her a crooked smile. "And I'll beat up anyone who gives you a hard time."

She laughed because she knew he was mostly joking.

OWEN WAS COMPLETELY OUT OF HIS ELEMENT. HE'D BEEN to work events with Evelyn before, but not like this. She'd told him it was a networking event, but he didn't really get what she meant. Now, being in the middle of it, he still didn't quite get it. People huddled together talking, then they split off and wandered to another group.

There were a few guys that he pegged as big-name people even though he didn't know them, simply because so many people flocked to be around them. Evelyn didn't.

"If that's the guy with all the money, why not pitch to him?" he asked as she surveyed the room.

"Because everyone is rattling off pitches to them. I'll be lost in a sea of mediocrity. They have so many things crossing their desks, it's hard to stand out."

"Sounds like you're afraid. If your idea is as good as you say it is, go big."

She smiled. "I can send a pitch to them whenever. I don't think face time makes a difference with them. They expect a whole lot of fawning that I'm not thrilled with. I don't want to kiss their asses when I know there's less than a five percent chance of them actually paying attention to me."

He listened and then looked closely at the interactions in those pools of people. Evelyn approached this with a precision he hadn't expected. "What's your plan?"

"I want to get face time with the midrange guys. Not someone small potatoes, but not a giant either. Those guys are still willing to take chances, and they have the money and backing to follow through."

"Lead the way."

He followed her through the room as she assessed where everyone was and created a plan for interacting with each of the people on her list of targets. In the first group they attached to, Evelyn practically elbowed her way in. "Kyle!" she said with fake cheer. "How have you been?"

"Good. Congratulations on the Women in Media award. I'm sorry I couldn't be there that night."

"Thanks. I got your email. That was thoughtful."

Their conversation had others backing off, and Owen wanted to follow, but he'd promised her that he'd be there for support. She reached behind her for his hand and introduced him. "Kyle, this is my significant other, Owen."

Owen swallowed the snort. Significant other. *I guess these people are too good to simply be called a boyfriend.* He reached past Evelyn. "Nice to meet you."

Kyle shook his hand. "What show do you work on?"

"I don't."

"Owen's not in the business. He's a firefighter."

"Wow. Really?" Kyle's eyes went wide. "I love watching Chicago Fire."

Owen clenched his jaw and gave a quick nod. He'd only watched the show once because Evelyn had made him. Then she'd gotten irritated when he'd corrected anything they got wrong.

"How's Trent Talks these days?" Kyle asked, turning his attention back to Evelyn.

"Good," she said, "but I'm leaving. I'm ready to move on to something different. I thought maybe we could talk about some ideas I have." She was smooth. Owen would give her that. While she launched into her pitch, he took her empty glass to let her know he'd get a refill so she could keep talking. While he waited to get the bartender's attention, a few people near him were talking about movies.

He listened, thinking maybe it was a conversation he could enjoy. Unfortunately, within a minute he realized that these people turned even a simple conversation about movies into a discussion of everything technical. One was discussing the camera angles used in a particular shot and how much more impact the opposite angle would have given the moment. Another chimed in that the angle was perfect because it showed just enough of the two leads to enthrall the audience, but the score had been off. They should've had a slower piece of music. No one wanted to see the characters have speed sex. Owen turned his laugh into a cough, which wasn't totally convincing, but caught the attention of the bartender.

He placed his order, and after grabbing his beer and Evelyn's champagne, he turned to find her. Kyle was talking to someone else now, so he scanned the room. He saw her in a dimly lit corner, standing too close to some other guy.

As he neared with the drinks, he couldn't hear their conversation. They spoke more quietly than those around them, making Evelyn lean closer. Then she did one of those over-the-top giggles, patting the man's chest. The caveman in Owen reared up. He did not like seeing her touch some other guy.

He held the glass out to Evelyn, which she accepted with a smile. She didn't stop the conversation to introduce him, however. She continued to laugh at whatever grandiose story the guy was telling. Owen listened for a minute and gathered it had something to do with a bungee jump gone wrong.

Everything Evelyn was doing was phony, but the man across from her obviously couldn't tell. After pretending to catch her breath from her bout of laughter, she reached out and touched the guy's arm. "Thank you for sharing that story, Adam. I'm going to chat with some other people. Definitely give me a call if you want to know more about my pitch."

"It was great catching up. I'll give you a call next week. Maybe we can have lunch and brainstorm some possibilities."

"Sounds good," she answered cheerfully. That part was sincere.

As she took Owen's arm, she leaned over and said, "Thank God you showed up with my drink. Adam is a one-trick pony. He only tells the one story about his adventurous life."

"So why bother?"

She sipped her champagne. "Because he's a guy who gets things done."

Owen grunted.

"What?"

"I don't see any male producers flirting to get face time with someone."

She pulled them to a stop. "First, you have no idea who here is pitching and who isn't. Second, I'm not flirting. Any idiot can see I'm here with you. But I do have to be friendly. Otherwise, I'm branded a bitch. Unfair? Of course. But it's the nature of the business. Changes are happening, but not nearly fast enough."

He bit down on his immediate response. He didn't like any of it—not that she flirted and someone might take it as an offer, not that because she was a woman she was expected to play nice instead of just going after what she wanted, not that he had no way of helping.

Swallowing down his jealousy and anger, he said, "Who's next?"

"I think Peter Garvey is a good prospect." She pointed across the room, near the bar where Owen had just been standing. "He heads the studio, but his wife pushes projects on him." She glanced around. "I wonder if Tricia is here."

For the rest of the night, Owen spent his time following in Evelyn's wake, grinding his teeth because she barely spoke to him, other than to make brief introductions.

When the night was finally winding down, he offered to get the car so she could say her goodbyes and meet him outside. He needed fresh air and distance from people. He let the cool breeze from the lake coast over him.

He paid for parking and drove around the block to come to the front of the building. He pulled in alongside a row of cabs to wait for Evelyn. He'd give her a few minutes and then text if she didn't come out. Going back in was out of the question. Even if he could stomach another round of TV people, he didn't want to risk the ticket for parking in a loading zone.

He trained his eyes on the entrance. Evelyn pushed through the door, but she wasn't alone. Adam escorted her out. Then he leaned over and kissed her. A quick brush of his lips against her cheek, but Owen saw red. He honked the horn to get her attention and then gripped the steering wheel. A moment later, Evelyn climbed in, Adam still at her back holding the door open. Damn, he should've gotten out of the car to open the door for her.

As she buckled up, Adam bent and looked at Owen. "It was great to meet you. Take care of our girl here."

"Will do." He couldn't force a smile or any other words. The man closed the door, and Owen tore out of the spot and toward the highway.

"Whew," she said as she kicked off her shoes and leaned back in her seat.

He didn't respond.

She sat up again. "Something wrong?"

"No." The word came out sharply.

"Yeah, that's believable."

He looked at her from the corner of his eye while he turned on the on-ramp. "I hated tonight."

"I know it's not your usual way of spending a night out, but it was important to me."

"That's the only reason my fist didn't run into Adam's face."

"What?"

"It's bad enough that you flirted with so many of those asshats. But it shouldn't be okay for them to touch you."

"You mean that kiss on the cheek as we were leaving? There was nothing inappropriate about that. I've known Adam a long time, and while we're not close, we're friendly."

"How friendly?"

"Go to hell. Do you think I'd bring you to an event to introduce you to past lovers?"

"I'm just wondering what happens at the parties I'm not at if there's that much going on right in front of me."

"Unbelievable," she muttered.

They dropped into silence, which was fine with him. He didn't like where the conversation was heading. When he changed lanes to get off the highway toward his house, she simply said, "I'd prefer to go home tonight. Alone."

He continued on to her condo. He parked but didn't get out to walk her up.

She slipped her shoes back on and opened the door. Before getting out, she turned to face him. "You need to get a few things straight. One, I am not Stacy. I wouldn't cheat on you—in your face or behind your back. Two, my job requires a lot of networking and talking to people and being friendly. If you can't handle that, there's no hope for us. I'm not going to give up my career for you."

She stepped out of the car and closed the door.

Owen watched as she walked inside. Even after she was gone, he continued to stare at the building. He'd screwed up. He slammed his fist into the steering wheel. He turned off the engine and went inside, even though Evelyn had made it clear she was done with him tonight. He got upstairs and knocked on her door. She didn't answer, so he knocked again. Just as he was about to use his key, the door opened. She stood in the opening, blocking his entrance.

"What do you want?"

"I'm sorry."

She let go of the door and stepped back.

"I know you're not Stacy, but it made me crazy watching you flirt—"

Her eyebrow winged up.

He held up a hand. "I know you weren't flirting. *I*

could tell it was phony. But they didn't know it. It grated on my nerves all night. Then when I saw Adam kiss you, I started to lose grip on my control." He reached out and touched her jaw. "I won't share you, but I would never expect you to give up your job. I have to find a way to live with seeing that and not letting my mind go where it did."

"I know you have hang-ups. We all have baggage. But until tonight, I never thought you looked at me as if I were Stacy."

"I don't."

"If not, why were you upset because some guy kissed my cheek? That's all it was. Would you act that way if it had been Gabe or Trevor?"

"No." His immediate thought was that they wouldn't do that to him. But neither would Evelyn. He knew that. "I don't know how to explain. I know it's irrational. I promise to work on it. I'm really sorry if I ruined your night."

She smiled. "Thank you." She hitched a thumb over her shoulder. "Want to come in?"

"As much as I'd love to, I have to get home to Probie."

"Okay. See you tomorrow?"

"Absolutely." He leaned in and kissed her, making sure it was nothing like any touch she'd received from anyone else all night.

As he drove home, the thoughts she had thrown out for consideration dogged him. Since his marriage and divorce, Evelyn was the only woman to gain his trust. But that was before they'd started sleeping together.

None of that mattered. Evelyn did. He trusted her, even if his behavior didn't reflect it.

Owen was on shift, so Evelyn went to Sunny's to meet her friends alone. She was still feeling off-center. As soon as she walked through the door of the diner, Nina practically screamed across the room.

"It's about time. Get your behind over her and give us details."

Tess shook her head as she sipped her coffee. Evelyn crossed to the table and sat. "Where are the guys?"

"On their way, I'm sure," Nina said with a wave of her hand. "Why didn't you tell us?"

"What?"

"Oh my God. You and Owen. We've been waiting for more than a year for the two of you to wake up and realize you're in love. When did this happen?"

Nina spoke so fast, Evelyn struggled to keep up. "Uh…"

Tess passed her a cup of coffee. "Take a breath and then tell us whatever you'd like to share." The look she gave Nina was a standard mom back-off look.

Evelyn took a drink of coffee and then a deep breath. So much had been happening with her and Owen that she hadn't realized that she hadn't seen her friends.

"Okay. The night of the awards ceremony I kissed him."

"Ooo…tell me more," Nina said with her chin in her hand.

"He rejected me because he thought I was drunk."

"Ouch."

"Not really. Anyway, a couple of days later, we talked and we admitted that something has been changing between us."

Nina smirked. "About time."

"How are things going?" Tess asked, ignoring Nina's comment.

"Pretty good, I guess."

Tess scrunched her face. "That sounds like you guys have already left the honeymoon phase."

"There's just so much happening. We had a great time at his brother's wedding. Although it was a little weird not having separate rooms. When we got back, I left my job. I'm searching for a new one."

"Wait. What?" Tess practically screeched.

"My boss wanted me to do more emotionally charged episodes, like the school shooting one. I refused right before the wedding. He thought I'd change my mind. I didn't. But it's okay. I'm pitching a new show to a lot of people."

Trevor and Gabe came in then.

"What'd we miss?" Trevor asked.

"I'll catch you up later," Tess said. Turning to Evelyn, she said, "Go on."

"I need some advice. Like I said, things have been really good between me and Owen. We went to a networking thing last night. I scored an invitation with the intention of making connections for my new show idea. He was my plus-one, as usual." She looked at Nina.

"By the time we left, though, Owen was pissed. He accused me of flirting with everyone I spoke to."

"Were you?" Gabe asked.

"Don't be a dick," Nina countered. "She would never do that to anyone, much less Owen."

"But would it look like flirting to Owen?" Gabe clarified.

Evelyn thought back to her interactions. She'd done nothing wrong. Nothing even hinted at trying to hook up with someone.

"I think what Gabe is trying to say and failing at, is that given Owen's history, he's overly sensitive to anything that might look like cheating," Trevor said.

"Just because his ex-wife cheated doesn't mean every woman on the planet is like that."

"And I'm sure logically, he knows that. There are still going to be things that will push his buttons," Trevor said.

"Am I supposed to be a nun?"

"No one is saying that," Gabe answered. "You know Owen. Things are black-and-white with him. He can trust you or he can't. Think about how you acted. How it would look to him. If something looks like a duck and walks like a duck..."

"Still being a dick, Gabe," Nina said.

"Don't you see what's going on here? Their whole relationship could blow up over some bullshit. What happens to us when they screw it up?" Gabe looked from Nina to Evelyn.

"We're not going to blow up." She couldn't imagine anything that would ruin her and Owen. Unless she actually cheated on him, which she would never do. "I acted no different than I have at any other event we've attended together."

"That was before you were sleeping together."

"What does that have to do with anything?"

"Do I really have to spell it out for you? The minute you changed your relationship, you became his. In the past, he might not have liked you flirting, but he had no claim on you."

She let his words sink in. What he said made sense, even though she balked at the idea of belonging to anyone. She studied Gabe for a moment. Something was off with him—more off than usual. "What's going on?"

"Nina's stupid challenge." He turned his glare on Nina. "I did what you said. I went out and met a woman at a bar. We drank, we talked, we fucked. Then she left without leaving me her number. When I looked her up, guess what I found?"

"Oh no," Evelyn said.

"She's married." He pointed at Nina. "That's why I look into people before I let them in my life."

"I said go out and meet people. Get to know them. Preferably before you stick your dick in them. Do you not remember that part? I never said go forth and have sex. We all know you have that ability."

"On that note, I'm out of here. I have to get to a job," Trevor said as he tossed some bills on the table. Sliding his chair back into place, he said to Gabe, "You don't get to blame her for your bad choices."

Nina stuck her tongue out at Gabe.

Trevor left, and Tess stood as well. "I have a patient to get to, but Trevor is right, Gabe. If you're going to try, then you have to change your approach." She turned to Evelyn. "Talk to Owen. He's level-headed."

When she was gone, Gabe said, "People suck."

"Not everyone," Evelyn said. "Look at Tess and Trevor. They found people. And you like us."

"You don't get input here. You're in love with your best friend. You didn't have to go out and find anyone. And I like you. Nina, I'm not so sure about."

Nina leaned over and hugged Gabe's arm. "You love me." He rolled his eyes.

Evelyn said, "I tried to find someone. I did the dating apps and coffee dates."

Straightening, Nina scoffed. "You did not try. You faked trying and then went home to Owen. There was no reason for you to look for someone when you were already in love."

She opened her mouth to argue that she hadn't been in love with Owen this whole time, but she stopped. Had she? Had her relationship with Owen prevented her from finding anyone else?

Nina grinned. "Man, I love being right."

When she left Sunny's, Evelyn was filled with things to think about. She considered the networking event and how it might've looked through Owen's eyes. She would never do anything to hurt him. Didn't he know that?

A COUPLE OF DAYS LATER, EVELYN WOKE IN OWEN'S BED. It was definitely a habit she could get used to. She was still having a hard time adjusting to not having to go to work. She hadn't been unemployed since college. She stretched out. Owen was gone. Sighing, she flipped back the covers. As she went downstairs, silence met her. Even Probie was gone, which meant Owen had gone for a run.

With a cup of coffee in hand, she went out to his front porch to wait for him. There was a slight chill in the air now that Chicago was barreling into fall, but the sun warmed her face. Her phone buzzed, disturbing her moment of peace.

"Hello," she answered after seeing it was Donald.

"Where are you?"

"Why?"

"I'm at your house. I have some good news."

"I'm at Owen's." Down the block, she saw Owen heading her way with Probie tugging at his leash.

"When will you be back here?"

"Not for a while," she said. Owen's face lit with a smile as he neared.

He unhooked Probie's leash, and the dog poked his cold nose at her before running up the stairs. Owen bent and kissed her head. He was sweaty from his run but looked good.

Donald huffed. "I have someone who is interested in producing your show."

That caught her attention, so she tore her eyes away from Owen, who was standing in the grass stretching his body. "What?"

"Marcus Dielman is expanding his studio in

Chicago. I mentioned you're in the market, and he wants to meet."

"Wow. Thank you. When?"

"I'm only in town tonight. I'll make reservations. Eight o'clock work for you?"

"Yeah."

They disconnected, and Evelyn sat in stunned silence. "Who was that?"

"Donald."

The muscle in Owen's jaw twitched.

"He's in town. He has a friend who might be interested in producing my show."

"Yeah? That's great."

"That was not the enthusiastic answer I hoped for." She stood to look him in the eye.

He stepped closer. "I'm glad someone wants your show. I just wish it wasn't connected to your ex."

"He's just making the introductions. Come with me. We're having dinner tonight. You can meet Marcus and help me woo him. Plus, you'll get to see that Donald is totally harmless."

With his hands on his hips, he sighed. "I don't know that I'll ever see him as harmless, but if you want me there, I'll come."

"Excellent. Now go take your shower, and I'll buy you breakfast."

He swooped in, wrapping an arm around her waist, and pulled her close. "How about you join me in the shower?"

"Tempting. Go warm it up. I'll be there in a minute."

He jogged up the stairs and led Probie into the house.

Evelyn sent Donald a text to make the reservations for four instead of three because Owen was joining them.

Is that a good idea?

Why not?

He's not in the business. You need to focus.

Owen will be there to support me, not as a distraction.

I hope so. This is a business meeting, not a group date.

Evelyn paused because his text rubbed her wrong. She hadn't implied it should be a date. She wanted to shoot something back that would be entirely inappropriate, like the middle finger emoji, but then she remembered that Owen was upstairs waiting. Hot naked man won every day over trading petty texts with her ex.

OWEN DIDN'T KNOW HOW EVELYN HAD ROPED HIM INTO doing this. They'd known each other for years, and while he'd met Donald on occasion, they'd never spent any time together. There was a good reason for that. Evelyn had shared plenty of stories over the years of how Donald was manipulative. Like the time he convinced her not to take a job working on a show because it would be bad for her career, only to snag the spot for himself. She'd justified forgiving him because she'd gotten an even better offer. Sometimes the manipulation wasn't even directed at her. He'd been known to screw people out of meetings with someone so he could take the spotlight. Everything was always about him. It was just how the man was wired.

Owen couldn't stand it. The pretense drove him crazy. He didn't trust a damn thing about Donald. He only looked out for number one, and if Evelyn got hurt, she was just collateral damage.

Owen wouldn't let that happen.

So, for her, he wore a suit. Again. Waited for her to get ready. Again. Except this time, he sat on the edge of her bed and watched her dress and primp. She wasn't sexy Evelyn tonight. She was all business, but the black skirt was just short enough to give him ideas. She swept the sides of her hair up and clipped it in place.

He rose and stood behind her. Scooping the rest of her hair to the side, he kissed her neck. He loved that his lips made her shiver. She closed her eyes and leaned against him.

"We have to get going," she murmured.

"I know. I'm ready. Your neck was too tempting for me to ignore."

She smiled and pulled away. "For the rest of the evening, I need you to ignore it. I'll make it worth your while when we get back here."

"You sure you want me to come? I can stay here and wait for you."

"I know you don't like the business stuff I do. All the schmoozing gets under your skin. But this is a good opportunity for you to see me and Donald together and understand that we are nothing more than friends."

He understood what she wanted, but he couldn't imagine a world in which he liked her ex. He could at least try not to be hostile toward him, though. "Okay. Let's go and get you a job."

They left her condo and walked to his car. As they pulled out into the street, he said, "Not to put a damper on this meeting, but what if he doesn't bite? Then what?"

"What do you mean?"

He didn't know how to phrase the rest without coming off like a condescending jerk, but he was worried about her. "If this guy doesn't want your show, what will you do?"

"I'll continue to shop it." She tilted her head and studied him. "What do you really want to know?"

"Are you okay on money? You left your job without having another lined up."

One corner of her mouth lifted. "I'm okay. I have money saved. I'm not going to be homeless any time soon."

"I'd never let you be homeless."

"That's very kind. But I don't need you to take care of me, either."

"I know."

He drove the rest of the way to the restaurant listening to her practice her pitch. He wasn't used to seeing her nervous. She always acted like she could handle anything. Whenever she participated in a party, a meeting, a conversation, she owned it. He parked near the restaurant and cut the engine. "Ready?"

"I better be." Her smile looked manic.

"Don't let them rattle you. Like you said, you just started pitching. There are a lot of other people out there. If this guy doesn't want it, someone else will. Then you can give him the big fuck-you."

Her burst of laughter echoed through the car. "Thank you. I can always count on you to deliver some perspective. Let's do this."

They entered the restaurant together, and Evelyn went to the hostess stand. "Hi. We're here for the Millhouse party."

"The rest of your party is already seated. Right this way."

"Shoot. Have they been here long?"

The woman shook her head. "Just a few minutes. They haven't even ordered drinks yet."

"Thank you."

Owen followed them to the table, where Donald was already deep in conversation with another man. He looked like he was trying to sell the guy a car. Or the Brooklyn Bridge. Owen took a deep breath. He'd promised Evelyn to at least try tonight. Both men stood when Evelyn reached the table. She extended a hand. "Hi, I'm Evelyn. You must be Marcus." They shook, and Donald came around to kiss her cheek.

Owen nodded a greeting before Donald went back to his own seat. Owen pulled the chair out for Evelyn and then introduced himself.

A waiter immediately stepped up and took their drink orders. Then the small talk started. They placed the order for their food before the subject of Evelyn's pitch was even broached. He didn't understand why they all needed to dance around. They'd set the meeting, and the purpose was clear.

Marcus said, "Tell me a little about what you've been working on."

"I've been with Trent Talks for more than eight years. I started as an assistant and worked my way up."

"Why are you looking to move?"

"I'm ready for a change. I know the Chicago market, and I've been thinking about this show for a long time. I believe now is the time to act."

"Tell me about the episode that won you the Women in Media award."

Her shoulders stiffened, and Owen laid a hand on her thigh. Her smile was barely an upturn of her lips. "We did an episode on the school shooting last year. It was pretty heart-wrenching."

"I told Evie it would be a hit. And look, now she's an award-winning producer." Donald sat back with a grin.

Owen gritted his teeth.

"It was a difficult show to get through. It's part of the reason why I'm looking to do something lighter. While that type of show has its place, it's not for me to produce."

"Tell me about what you envision this talk show to be."

She opened her mouth, but Donald cut her off. "She has six months' worth of episodes lined up. I've seen the host. She's polished but not Hollywood."

After a deep breath, she said, "Marilyn grew up here in the city. She's connected to people through business and the charity work she does. People genuinely like her."

"I think we could have a real winner on our hands here, Marcus."

Why the fuck doesn't Donald shut up?

"What do you mean, we?" she asked.

"Didn't Donald tell you? We're thinking about working together on this project. Is that a problem?"

"Of course not," she said with another forced smile. "The important thing is getting the show to air."

Of course not? Owen took a drink to try to swallow down his anger. Didn't she see how manipulative Donald was being? It was one thing to make an introduction, another to invite himself on board for her project.

"I've put some feelers out and had some conversations. Prime morning would be difficult."

Without giving her a chance to respond, Donald jumped in. "The best time to air is early morning. Get the audience involved so they're talking about us when they get to work."

Smoothing her napkin on her lap, she waited for Donald to finish. "I agree with Marcus. I think going up against the Today Show or Good Morning America would be a tough sell. They have their audience, and while we might be able to snag a few viewers, we're not going to be providing the same entertainment. I can send you the market research I have."

Marcus leaned forward. "You have market research?"

"I have friends at a number of studios who were willing to share. I've done my homework. The ebb and flow of what people want is swaying again. I believe now is a good time. Audiences are ready for this kind of show."

Owen felt a swell of pride. It didn't matter what Donald pulled. She held her own, not allowing him to muscle his way through what she wanted.

Dinner arrived, and conversation turned again to more mundane things. Evelyn continued to slide in information about Chicago, people who would make good guests, and the angle she'd take with them. He enjoyed seeing this side of her. The side that was on target and a little cutthroat. It was damn sexy.

Chapter Eight

When dinner was finished, Marcus left his card with Evelyn, and she tucked it into her purse. *Take that, Donald. I don't need you to play go-between.* Owen excused himself to go to the bathroom. While Donald took care of the check, she leaned forward and said sharply, "What the hell was that all about?"

"What?" He actually had the nerve to look innocent.

"First, you ran over the top of me every time I attempted to have a conversation—"

"I just wanted to make sure you didn't put your foot in your mouth and ruin a good thing."

"Are you serious? You just did it again. I'm totally capable of talking to people and pitching my show. I've been doing this a long time. And to my second point, what is this about you partnering with Marcus? You didn't mention anything about that."

"I didn't want you to refuse the meeting because I might be part of the project. Especially since you brought Owen. I think we all know how he feels about me."

"You told me you had this great new gig. What happened with that?"

"Nothing. It's a limited-run evening special. If it hits big, they'll probably extend it, but I'm keeping my options open."

Owen returned but didn't even sit. "Ready?"

"More than." She stood and said to Donald, "I'm sure I'll be seeing you soon."

Donald stood, buttoned his jacket, and said, "Can I have a minute?"

Owen's fingers flexed on her lower back. He was being so good tonight.

She looked at him over her shoulder. "Can you get the car? I'll be right out."

"Fine."

Donald came around the table to walk her to the door. "I'm not trying to piss you off, Evie."

"Please stop calling me that."

He sighed as if she were being insufferable. "I want you to get your show. You deserve it. I have faith in you, and the more people you have backing you, the more likely it'll be that the show will run."

"I don't like the omissions, that's all. And I don't want you to be a part of this if you think our relationship means you can tell me how to produce the show."

He chuckled. "Relationship or not, as executive producer, that's exactly what it means."

"You're not funny."

"We make a good team, Ev—Evelyn."

"We'll see. I didn't offer Marcus an exclusive. I'm still pitching."

Owen pulled up in front. She turned and extended a hand to Donald so he got the hint. He shook his head and then took her hand. "I hope he knows how special you are."

"He treats me better than anyone ever has."

"Ouch."

"See you later." She walked to the car and got in. "Thank you," she said to Owen when he pulled out into traffic.

"For what?"

"Everything. Coming to this boring dinner. Not punching Donald. Going to get the car even though you didn't want to leave me alone with him. Thank you for being you."

"You're welcome. I'd do anything for you." They drove in silence for a few minutes. Then he said, "What the hell is up with that guy anyway?"

"Donald?"

"How did you stay married to him? He talked over you like you weren't even there. And he's going to be your boss now?"

"Not my boss. It's not a done deal. There's something going on. With Donald, there always is. He won't let me know until it's useful for him to do so." She reached across the car and stroked the back of his head. "When we were saying goodbye he asked if you're good to me. I told him no one has ever treated me better."

He barked out a laugh. "That's mean. But I like it." He took her hand and kissed it.

With a man like Owen at her side, she had no more

worries about whether she could do this. They truly made a good team. She loved that he believed in her. Owen didn't question her ability or how she approached things. And he listened when she spoke.

Until now, she had no idea how fulfilling it was to have a true partner.

OVER THE NEXT WEEK, EVELYN HAD FOUR LUNCH meetings and two coffee dates to pitch her show. For the first time in years, she felt completely talked out. She sat in Owen's living room working on the next round of contacts and emailing everyone she'd met with this week. Owen was at the youth center. They were having a fund-raiser all weekend. He'd been there pretty much every hour possible. He was worried because the budget had been cut and usual charitable contributions hadn't come through.

She tapped her pen against her notebook in thought. Owen cared more about the center than anything else in his life. He loved being a firefighter, but working at the center gave him the chance to impact the lives of kids. She wished she could do more to help.

An idea suddenly struck. She was planning a TV show based on the premise that Chicago was a great place. Why not highlight the center and its impact on the neighborhood and the kids it served?

She jotted down some ideas and then paused. Owen had been really upset when she did the school shooting episode of *Trent Talks* because he thought she was exploiting the kids. He was right. Would this be the same?

Her phone rang, and she almost ignored it because the thought of having another conversation made her head hurt. The screen showed Marcus's name, so she answered. "Hello, this is Evelyn."

"Hi, Evelyn. It's Marcus Dielman."

"How are you, Marcus?"

"Good. I hope even better in a few minutes."

Her heart picked up. If he were just calling for more information, he'd blurt it out. This was the call. An offer.

"Yes?"

"I want your show. I would've called sooner, but I wanted to make sure I had the studio space and a place for it."

Her breath caught. A place? That was almost too fast. "You mean you have a slot on TV for it?"

"Assuming we can come to terms on a contract, yes."

He continued to talk, but Evelyn had a hard time hearing him. A buzz filled her head. She stood and shook her body out. "I'm sorry. Can you repeat that?"

"How about I have the contract emailed to you? Take a look and let me know what you think."

"What about Marilyn? Do you want to meet her?"

"Of course. Let's work on getting you on board officially and then we'll deal with Marilyn. If she's half as good as you sold her as, we shouldn't have any problems. Do you have any questions?"

"Only about a million. But they can keep for now. Thank you."

"Don't need to thank me. Bring me a good show. Look for the contract in your inbox shortly."

"I will." She disconnected and opened her email. She refreshed three times before she realized how ridiculous she was being. She knew better than to get too excited. It might be a shit offer.

Instinct had her wanting to call Owen, but he was busy with the center. He didn't need an interruption. Plus, she needed to talk to Marilyn. While another host might work for the show, she really wanted Marilyn. She resisted pressing the button next to Owen's name and scrolled to Marilyn's number instead.

"Hi, Evelyn. How's it going?"

"Excellent. I have an offer for the show."

"You do?"

"I don't have all the details and although they'll want you to come in, they're looking for me to sign on first. I'll know more when I get my contract, but I plan to do everything in my power to make sure you're part of the package. That is, assuming you still want to?" She paced the room to work off the nervous energy.

Probie followed her back and forth, almost like he was waiting for her to drop some food. His nails clicked on the hardwood floor, keeping time with her steps.

"Is the show still like we talked about?"

"As far as I know. I pitched it the same."

"Then I'm in. It'll be exciting to do something different."

Marilyn was a busy woman who was involved with more charities than Evelyn even knew existed.

"What about your other obligations?"

A trickle of laughter sounded across the line. "I don't

have too many obligations. I do what I want, when I want. When people call and ask for my help, I get involved if I'm free. Having my own show just means that I say no more often." The laughter increased. "My own show. That sounds crazy. It's crazy, isn't it?"

She stopped and Probie crashed into her legs, almost knocking her over. "Not crazy. Everyone has to start somewhere. I just wanted to let you know that we have some forward motion. Even if this offer isn't great, we can use it to leverage another."

"How about I let you handle all of that, and you just tell me what to do?"

"As soon as I get the contract, I'll have more information, but based on what Marcus said, they're looking to move on this. They even have a time slot for the show."

Marilyn whistled. "So this is really happening."

"Unless the contract is ridiculous."

"Awesome. I'm looking forward to learning more."

They said goodbye, and Evelyn was still filled with nervous energy. "Come on, Probie. Let's go for a walk."

She grabbed the leash and hoped the dog didn't think she was going to run the way Owen did. A walk would get rid of her excess energy, and she could stop for a bottle of champagne to celebrate with Owen when he got home.

OWEN DRAGGED HIMSELF UP THE FRONT STEPS AND walked into the house. As long as his weekend had been at the center, something in him perked up with the knowledge that Evelyn was here waiting for him. He remembered what she'd said about having someone to come home to. He hadn't even considered how much he'd missed it until right now.

In the living room, she had a few candles lit and a bottle of champagne sitting on the table. "Evelyn?"

She came from the kitchen. "You're home." The smile on her face was wide and infectious.

He smiled in return without having a reason to. "What's this all for?"

"To celebrate."

He stared at the bottle. The fund-raising efforts this weekend were a relative flop. He had nothing to celebrate.

"Marcus wants my show," she explained.

Over the past few weeks, she'd mentioned so many different names, he took a minute to scan his memory.

"Donald's connection," she provided. "He's going to send a contract, so it's not a done deal, but I'm so excited to have real interest. He wants it. He already has a time slot for us."

"Congratulations." He pulled her into a hug. "Does this mean you're working with Donald all the time?"

He tried to keep his question emotionless because he knew he shouldn't be jealous of her ex, but the man annoyed the hell out of him. He couldn't imagine having Donald be a regular part of their lives.

"If he partners with Marcus, he'll technically be my boss. But that doesn't mean he'll be working with me regularly. They make sure the money is there and line up the advertising. They'll give some direction on the show, kind of like Harry did."

"This makes you happy?"

"If the contract is good, yeah."

"Then I'm happy for you."

"Even if it comes with Donald?"

He shrugged. "If he's your boss, he won't be able to touch you or hit on you or it'll be harassment."

She laughed and pressed forward to kiss him. Then she poured them each a glass of champagne. "To success."

They clinked and drank. When they settled on the couch, she asked, "How did everything go at the center?"

"Not good. Turnout was lower than we hoped for, and the money is trickling in. We need more of a waterfall." He leaned back, and she tucked in next to him.

"I've been thinking about the center. How would you feel about me highlighting the center on my new show?"

"What do you mean?"

She set her glass on the table and twisted to face him. "I know how protective you are of the kids, and I know my sense of things is a little skewed based on my job. So before I continue, please trust that this isn't about ratings or exploiting your kids."

His neck prickled warily. The only way she would preface a conversation like that was if she thought she might be crossing a line, like she did last year. He swallowed. "Go ahead."

"The new show is supposed to be Chicago-centric. I want to show the good side of the city. The youth center is one of those good things. I have a five-part series planned out. It wouldn't be the whole episode but a segment each day showing a piece of what the center does. It would bring awareness and with that attention, hopefully money."

He waited, thinking there was something else, some catch. Nothing came. "That's it?"

"Well, I have a list of ideas. Like we could do one segment on the sports teams you coach. Another day on the art and tech classes offered. Showcase the students who received scholarships for college. We can interview adults who came up through the center."

He listened to her talk and realized that she was mentioning things he hadn't discussed with her. "How do you know about all that?"

"I did my homework. I know how important the center is to you. I want to help."

His throat tightened. No one had ever stepped up for him like this before. "That would be amazing."

She released a long breath. "I thought you might be mad."

"Because you want to help the center?"

She snuggled close to him again. "I thought you might think I planned to use the center to launch the next phase of my career."

"I'm not against using something for your career as long as it's mutually beneficial. That school shooting episode of Trent Talks didn't benefit anyone except the show."

"It brought a wider awareness of the long-term consequences of a shooting."

He hated that she still tried to defend that show.

"Awareness had nothing to do with it. You wanted to make people cry. You used kids like mine to do it."

"And you know I hated that part of it. That's why I almost didn't bring this up to you."

"You think you can make it happen?"

"It's my job to plan the shows. I'm sure in the beginning I'll have to bring it to Marcus and Donald, but this is exactly the type of episode I pitched to them."

"You're an amazing woman, you know that?"

She climbed onto his lap. "Yes, I am quite the catch. It's nice of you to notice."

Gripping her hips, he held her snug against him. "And oh so humble."

She lowered her mouth to his. She tasted like the champagne they shared. He could sip on her forever. He loved what their relationship was becoming.

He loved her. Was in love with her.

Reaching up, he pushed her hair back so he could see her whole face when he said the words. "I love you."

She smiled. "I love you, too."

He blew out a breath. When you loved someone as long as he had loved her, how was he supposed to say it in a way to make her realize that this was different? "No, Evelyn. I'm in love with you. More than as a friend. More than as a lover. I love you with my whole heart. You've managed to seep into every cell of my body in a way no one else will ever be able to erase. I'm yours."

She blinked back tears. "For a guy who doesn't like to talk, you seem to know exactly what to say to turn my world upside down." She smiled again. "I love you, too. All of me. Forever." She leaned forward to meet his lips. Against his mouth, she whispered, "No one else."

Like somehow she knew he needed to hear the words.

Their kiss was hot and sexy, yet meaningful in a completely new way. Owen knew he wouldn't have the words to describe it, so he didn't try. He simply let her take him to that place where they were perfect.

THE CONTRACT MARCUS SENT WAS PRETTY GOOD. THEY spent days going back and forth negotiating smaller points. They conceded and gave her voice in approving the host, which meant Marilyn was a shoo-in. She was comfortable enough with the terms that she didn't try to find a better offer.

Once the contract was signed, everything that had been moving like a sloth was now fast-forward. She'd been putting in long hours hiring a crew since Marcus was in New York.

He'd sent an assistant from his office to work with her. Tyler was young, but he'd been working with Marcus long enough that he knew what he was doing. This wasn't his first launch. And Evelyn was more than a little grateful Donald wasn't there.

While she knew she could work with Donald, it would upset Owen. They hadn't been seeing all that much of each other because of her long hours. At least Owen understood. Since he worked twenty-four-hour shifts, he wasn't sitting around waiting for her.

She'd dated some guys who'd call repeatedly

wondering when she'd be off work. Not Owen. He called and texted to check in and talk about their days. More often than not, when he was off, she spent the night at his house so they had some time together.

Unfortunately today, working with Donald was unavoidable. Marilyn was coming to the studio for a run-through audition. Then they were meeting to lay out the first few weeks of episodes.

It was really happening. She was going to air the first show she developed from the ground up. In the studio, they were using Marilyn's audition as a test run for the crew. She needed to see if the people they hired were a good fit both for the show and with one another.

Donald volunteered to be interviewed by Marilyn, so once the lights were set and the cameras ready, they started.

"Hi, Donald. It's so nice to have you here today. For those in our audience who don't know who you are, can you tell us a little about yourself?"

"I'm your boss, one of the executive producers of the show."

In Marilyn's ear, Evelyn said, "Don't let him rattle you. It's a test. Ask him something personal."

"What is something you're passionate about? What really gets your motor revved?"

Some of the crew snickered, and even Evelyn couldn't stop her laugh. With anyone else, the question probably would've been fine, but this was Donald.

"Success. Everything I do, every move I make, is designed to ensure I achieve the success I'm after."

"That's great in business, but what about your personal life?"

"It holds true in my private life as well. It's all about perspective. If I deem success to mean getting the girl, then I do everything in my power to make that happen."

Marilyn fanned herself. "Woof. Talk about being an alpha. What do you do when the woman wants no part of this definition of success?"

"That almost never happens. But I can respect what a woman wants. And if it's not me, I change my definition of success."

He stared into the camera and Evelyn felt it as if he were talking to her. She blinked to break the spell. She knew Donald had that effect on people. She'd witnessed him use that charm to get everything he wanted and to talk himself out of whatever jam he'd gotten into. It was a special kind of skill set.

She'd take Owen's straightforward attitude any day.

The director yelled, "Cut!" Marilyn leaned over and shook Donald's hand. "Thank you for that. I hope I didn't come across as too nervous." She pointed to the lights and camera. "It's a lot to take in."

Evelyn left the control room and made it to the stage, which was still under construction and design. "You did a great job. Don't play coy. You've been in front of cameras before."

"On the other end of the couch, sure. It's different when it's up to me to keep the conversation going. He didn't make it easy with his short responses."

"You did fine. With any other guest, we'd have a bio and questions prepared ahead of time. This was just about getting a feel for your stage presence."

They shared a quick hug, and Evelyn told her she'd call soon with news. Then Donald put his hand on her lower back and said, "Marcus is in the conference room. Let's talk."

Evelyn took a quick extra step to get out of his reach. She wouldn't go so far as to swat his hand away—she didn't need the gossip—but she didn't want him thinking it was okay to constantly touch her, either.

When they got to the conference room, Marcus was on a call, so they took a seat and waited.

"What did you think of Marilyn?" she asked.

"How much did you feed her through the earpiece?"

"Nothing. Other than to point out you were just being difficult to test her. I played fair."

He pursed his lips and tilted his head. "I taught you better than that. But if that's the case, you have a good eye."

Marcus finished his call. "Her instincts are better than good. I've whispered about the show to a few people, and it's already generating buzz."

"Without a name?" As far as she knew, the show was still untitled.

"We're going with Chi-talk Live. We've gotten enough feedback to let us know people react to the name and recognize it as something different. I want to start within two weeks, so let's talk details."

"Does that mean Marilyn is hired?"

"My assistant has already sent her the contract."

"Then why did she need to audition?" Evelyn looked at both men.

"We needed to see if she could hold her own in front of a camera. She'll get some practice in and smooth out her edges, but she did well. Let's talk about the first episodes."

Evelyn pulled out her portfolio. "I know I sent you a list of ideas, but I have something new to add to the list. A five-part series on a youth center in Chicago." She removed the page and handed a copy to Marcus and one to Donald.

Donald barely glanced at it. "Evie, this is nothing like what you pitched."

She didn't grind her teeth at the nickname that he wouldn't stop using, but she was completely confused. "This is perfect. The center has a huge, positive impact on the neighborhood and the families who live there."

He took a deep breath. "How can I put this delicately?" He looked to Marcus, who was still reading her notes, and then back at her. "These kids are a reminder of the downtrodden in society. We're supposed to be lighthearted and happy."

"But—"

Marcus looked up. "He has a point, Evelyn. I'm not saying we can never do something like this, but for the opening weeks, we need to nail it. We have to keep the audience laughing and coming back for more. If we start pulling on heartstrings, it'll be a tougher sell."

Evelyn's heart sank. At least it wasn't a no. It was a not-right-now. In a few months, or next season, she'd definitely be able to slide in at least a few segments for Owen and his kids.

Without any further discussion from Evelyn, Marcus continued. "We've gone through the list you originally provided and have pulled the topics and guests we think will draw the biggest market share. I've emailed it to you, so you can start lining up the guests. Any other questions?"

"Based on my contract and the conversations we've had so far, I was under the impression I would have some freedom to develop the episodes."

"And you will. My hand stays in the pot until we get the formula right. Once we get our format and brand down, you'll mostly be on your own."

She smiled. Owen had nothing to worry about. His center would get the spotlight. It was just going to take a little time.

OWEN GOT OFF SHIFT AND HOPED EVELYN WOULD STILL be at home when he got there. Home. He liked the idea of his house being hers. Unfortunately, she was already gone. Judging by the lack of coffee in the kitchen, she'd been gone for hours. When she got up not long before he got home, she normally left the pot on for him. She had left a note on the fridge, though.

Auditions and meetings all day in the studio. It's real! I might be late. Love, E

Setting up a new show was a lot of work. He'd seen the emails and spreadsheets and notes she'd been dealing with for weeks now. But she was happy. She was happier than he'd seen her in a long time, so he couldn't complain. And she never bitched about his hours. She might be the perfect woman. It was just another reminder of how well they fit into each other's lives.

He walked Probie and then took a nap. Later, he swung by the youth center and talked to Sandra about Evelyn giving them a spot on her new show. While he was there, he played a pickup game of basketball with the high school boys. He'd hoped to be able to get them new uniforms this year, but with the pitiful results of the fund-raiser, he doubted it would happen.

At home, he made tacos for dinner. Evelyn had texted to say she was on her way over. She arrived as he pulled food off the stove.

"How was your day?"

"So good. Marilyn's audition was excellent. As it turns out, it was just a test to make sure she could handle being in front of the camera and could shoot from the hip. I thought they'd want to bring in other possible hosts, but she's hired if they agree on contract terms. Since it's not about the money for Marilyn, I'm pretty sure she's going to sign. How about your day?"

"I napped. I went to the center. Sandra is thrilled with the idea of you doing segments on the center. Let her know what you need." He set food on the table.

Evelyn lost the sparkle she came in with. She shifted awkwardly. "About that."

"What?" He sat and pointed at the chair across from him and handed her a plate.

"I presented the segment ideas to Marcus and Donald."

Although he wanted to make a face when she said Donald's name, he didn't actually do it. *Point for me.*

"They shot me down."

"Why would they do that? I thought it was your show."

"They don't think it's feel-good or lighthearted enough for the first episodes." She dragged her chair closer to him and took his hand. "Next season, I'll be able to do it for sure."

"Next season? We need funding now. The budget has shrunk. People haven't donated. I was hoping that those segments would bring people out."

"I know. But Marcus and Donald have the money, so they have final decision. Once we have the groundwork laid and have built an audience, I'll have more freedom."

He slid his hand away. "Did you tell Donald this was important to me?"

She shrank back. "This has nothing to do with you. Or us. It was a business decision."

"I'd like to believe that, but when it comes to you, little with Donald seems to be only business." He pushed away from the table, his appetite gone.

While it wasn't Evelyn's job to save the youth center, she'd gotten his hopes up. Knowing that it was Donald who didn't want the segments to air made it feel personal. He needed air to clear his head. "I'm taking Probie for a walk."

He left without waiting for a response from Evelyn. The temperature was dipping as the full force of fall hit Chicago. The leaves were turning, falling, and blowing across the sidewalks. When he got back to the house, Evelyn was sitting on his front steps. He released Probie's leash, and the dog ran straight to her.

"Do you want me to go home?"

"No," he answered. "I know I shouldn't be mad at

you. Right now, it feels like you took Donald's side and that bugs me. This was really important, and he took it away. You let him. And before you give me that look, I know it's irrational."

"I feel bad about making an offer I can't uphold. *Yet*. I want to do the segments. I will do them." She took his hand. "In the meantime, I talked with Marilyn while you were gone. In addition to being the host of my new show, she is a world-class fund-raiser. She sits on the board of many foundations and stuff. She's always running something."

He walked toward the door, still holding her hand. "Are you going somewhere with this?"

"Marilyn is going to help the center. She said she'd put something together within the next month or so. The people she knows have deep pockets. It might not solve all the budget problems, but it'll be a start."

He held the door open for her, speechless.

"I know how important the center is to you. I didn't think Marcus would tell me no. Getting Marilyn involved is my way of saying I'm sorry for making a promise I can't keep right now."

He pulled her into his arms. "Have I told you how amazing you are?"

"It's been a while. Like at least twenty-four hours. Maybe you should show me."

"I'm sorry I got mad. It was mostly disappointment. I appreciate anything you can do for the center." He lowered his mouth to hers.

"If it's important to you, it's important to me. We're a team, right?"

He loved hearing her say that. "Absolutely."

Chapter Nine

Owen had been picking up extra shifts to earn more money that he could donate to the youth center. He'd been carrying extra weight for days. He said he didn't blame her, but Evelyn felt guilty. She wanted to do more for him. Especially since he'd made the news—well, not him, but the fire he'd been fighting.

She'd ordered dinner in, had already taken Probie on an extended walk, and had one of Owen's favorite black-and-white movies queued up on the TV. Tonight was going to be just about him. When he walked through the door, he looked worn out. The extra hours were taking a toll on him. Today's fire added to that burden.

"Hey," he said as he kicked off his shoes. "What're you doing here? Thought you'd be working."

Another pang of guilt struck. She *had* been working a lot. Trying to get the show up and running was no simple task.

Before she had a chance to answer, he said, "I'm sorry. That came out wrong. I know you've been busy." He hefted a sigh. "I'm not going to be very good company tonight." He dropped his bag and jacket on the chair.

"I wanted to see you." No. She needed to see him. When he stared at her, she continued, "The fire made the news, and I saw your truck on the scene. I knew you were working, but I didn't see you."

"You shouldn't watch things like that."

"I don't. Usually. But I was at the station and it came up on a screen in the background and I couldn't not look. How are you?" she asked softly.

"I'm fine. Just tired."

She sighed instead of saying, "Don't be stupid." She couldn't imagine how he'd be fine. Two kids had died in the fire. He was probably beating himself up for not finding them in time. It didn't matter that they had rescued twenty other people.

"I don't want to talk about it." As he walked past her, he kissed her head and kept moving.

"What can I do?" she asked.

"Nothing. Just go home. I'll call you tomorrow."

He headed toward the bedroom, and she sat for a minute. Sometimes, he was hard to read. Hell, most of the time he was. She wanted to help him, but he closed off. It looked like this was going to be one of those times she would have to push up against him, so she followed.

She stood in the doorway, leaning against the frame. "You don't get to push me away. I wouldn't let you do it when we were friends. I'm not going to let you do it now. Talk to me."

He was at the dresser, head down, hands fisted. "I can't."

She stepped closer and placed a tentative hand on his back. His muscles quivered beneath her touch. He rarely talked about his job and what he did. Sure, he was always quick with a funny story, but not the tough stuff. Not the calls that got to him.

Those he bottled up.

Evelyn knew he did it, but it wasn't until right now that she realized how hard that was. She stroked his back. His muscles bunched and flexed in response.

"You always take care of me. Everyone, really. Let me take care of you for a change." When her hand touched his side, he winced. He'd been hurt. "What happened?"

He straightened and shoved away from the dresser. "Not now, Evelyn. I can't."

When she looked into his eyes, she saw his torment. She tugged at his shirt and pulled it over his head. Sure enough, a bruise bigger than the span of her hand bloomed on his side. She leaned forward and kissed his chest. He trembled.

"Let me make you feel better," she whispered against his skin. If he wouldn't use words, she'd let him use his body.

He released a rough sigh. Then he gripped her upper arms and pushed her away. "I can't. Not like this. I—"

She saw it then. He was on edge, barely holding on to the tight control that he used to get through life. "You don't scare me, Owen. I know you won't hurt me. Use me to feel better. I'll give you anything you need."

The rapid rise and fall of his chest was the only indication that he'd heard her, that she was having any effect on him whatsoever.

"Go home," he said gruffly.

"No." She stood her ground.

He closed his eyes, so she made her move, getting close to him again. She touched his neck and slid her hand up to his hair. His eyes reopened on a growl. Knocking her hand away, he thrust both of his hands into her hair to hold her head. He kissed her hard then. They came together in a mashing of lips and teeth and tongues. He tightened his hold on her hair as his mouth moved down, and he bit the juncture where her shoulder and neck met.

Her nerves were on fire. This was the passionate Owen she remembered from their one night years ago. She hadn't even realized this version of him had been missing. While they'd been having great sex, this was off the charts. This was Owen open and raw. He didn't like anyone to see him this way.

She tugged at the button of his jeans and reached inside to stroke him. He grabbed her hand and pinned it behind her back. *Okay then. He wants to run this show.* She let him. He let go of her hair and her wrist to step away. The size of his pupils made his eyes nearly black.

"Ready to leave now?"

"Hell no," she answered. She yanked her shirt over her head and tossed it to the floor. "I said you don't scare me."

"I should."

"Never." She slid her pants down and stepped out of them. "If this is what you need to feel better, I'm here."

He closed his eyes again. She moved to her knees and pulled his jeans down, taking his underwear with them. She licked him from base to tip, swirled her tongue around the head, and then took him fully into her mouth. His groan sounded like a cross between frustration and relief. She became wet as he once again grabbed her head to guide the motion and pace he wanted. He fucked her mouth, and she moved one hand inside her panties to find her own release. When she moaned with his dick in her mouth, he suddenly reared back and picked her up off the floor.

He thrust his hand into her underwear and stroked her roughly, sending a tremor through her body. "Is this what you want?"

"God, yes." She braced her hands on his shoulders as he pressed two fingers into her.

Then he removed his hand, almost causing her to topple. "Take them off."

She pushed her underwear down while watching him. He licked his fingers. She undid her bra and tossed it. Her nipples were so hard, they hurt.

"Get on the bed."

She did as she was told, lying back, but propping herself up on her elbows. He kicked off the rest of his clothes. Then, without warning, he grabbed her ankles and slid her to the edge of the bed. He hit his knees and buried his face between her legs. The first stiff contact of his tongue against her clit had her body bowing over the bed.

An arm came down across her hips and pinned her to the mattress. The first orgasm ripped through her quickly. Her thighs trembled around his head as she tried to move. His grip was too tight, so she fisted the blanket and dug her heels into his back.

His tongue slowed, and he kissed her inner thigh. Evelyn swallowed and concentrated on slowing her breathing.

"How many times?" he asked gruffly.

"What?"

"How many times can you come?"

"I don't know."

"Tonight we're gonna find out."

"Owen." She struggled to push up on her elbows again. "I want to take care of you."

"You said you'd give me whatever I want." He bit her inner thigh. "I want this." He slid two fingers in her again and began a slow, torturous thrust.

His tongue danced all over her without touching her clit. Her whole body became riled up with need. She was on the brink of another orgasm when he pulled back. She forced her eyes open, but before she could attempt to move, he shoved her whole body farther up the bed. She heard the condom wrapper, and then he was over her and inside her.

He was licking and sucking her stiff nipples. She cried out in pleasure-pain. Her hands held his head as he moved from one nipple to the other while slowly thrusting, causing every nerve ending to feel his full length. New sensations assaulted her as she was close to coming but not quite there. She wrapped her legs around his hips in an effort to keep him close. She raised her hips to meet his thrusts. Anything to seek relief.

He took the hint and rose up. He spread her legs

wide and began to piston into her. He moved so fast, her entire body jostled and jiggled. He felt so good, but the frustration built to a peak. She slid a hand down to where they were joined. She wanted to come while he was inside her. She managed to barely bump her clit before he grabbed both her wrists and stretched them out over her head.

With one hand he pinned her there. His other hand reached under her and lifted her ass just a bit. "Please, Owen. I'm close."

He lowered his mouth to her ear, bit the lobe gently. "This is about me, remember?"

She wanted to cry. Her entire being was like a taut wire ready to snap. He just kept strumming and plucking her, though, keeping her orgasm out of reach.

He pulled completely out of her, and a new kind of frustration struck. She felt empty. He tapped her hip. "Roll over."

Her muscles were heavy and slow, but she pushed herself over, rising on her knees to press her ass against him. He slid home again, refilling her. She moaned into the pillow and grabbed the bars of his iron headboard.

He picked up the pace again. Sounds of flesh slapping mixed with his guttural moans. Then he curled his whole body around hers. One hand pinched a nipple while the other pinched her clit.

She was gone. She screamed and cried out. Her muscles trembled as her pussy gripped him and pulled him deeper. The lights behind her closed lids blinded her. She was vaguely aware of him pumping away into her and his teeth sinking into the back of her shoulder.

But she was no longer in control of anything. As if she ever had been.

At some point, he released her, and she collapsed. Her heart thundered and blood rushed so loud that she wasn't even sure if she was still conscious. She closed her eyes and just let her body relax.

OWEN STUMBLED OFF THE BED. *WHAT HAVE I DONE? FUCK.* He ripped the condom from his sensitive flesh. Staring at Evelyn's sweat-slicked back, he struggled to control his breathing.

She rolled over, her eyes barely open. He scanned her body again, taking note of the marks he'd left. "Fuck. I'm so sorry."

"For what?" she asked, her voice craggy like she had just woken up.

"Everything." He backed away.

"Come here." She waved at him and then patted the mattress beside her.

He didn't move.

"You're really going to make me move right now?" She huffed. She rolled halfway to the side and pushed herself to sitting. She reached out and took his hand. Tugging, she said again, "Come here."

"I've done enough."

"Says who?" she said with a wink.

She wasn't angry or scared? He sank to his knees in

front of her at the edge of the bed. He kissed her softly. "You shouldn't have let me."

She stroked his head and laughed. "Why the hell not? That was the hottest sex I've ever had. You've been holding out on me."

"How could you say you enjoyed that?" He touched the bite marks on her shoulder, the hickey on her breast.

Cradling his jaw, she forced him to look at her. She stared him in the eye for a few heartbeats before speaking. "I will never be afraid of you. You didn't hurt me. Not really. These marks? They just show that you wanted—needed—me so badly you finally lost control. It's okay to let go with me."

"You deserve better."

"You always take care of me. There's nothing wrong with what happened in this bed, Owen. If I'd wanted you to stop, I would've told you, and you would have." She kissed him gently.

He wanted to believe her. He wanted to believe she not only wasn't bothered by the hard fucking that they'd done, but she'd enjoyed it.

"Even if you hadn't just rocked my world with the most amazing orgasms, it would've been fine. It's okay to take what you need sometimes."

He pulled her hand away from his face. "It wasn't okay with Stacy. She got mad at me for leaving marks. Said she preferred me being gentle."

"I'm not Stacy. I love when you're gentle and you treat me like your whole world depends on my happiness and pleasure. But you get to have that feeling, too.

However you need to get there." Stroking his jaw again, she added, "I love you."

He studied her face. He knew when she was lying, but now she spoke the truth, and it was such a relief to him. She'd seen every part of him and she still wanted him, loved him. A lump settled in his throat, threatening to cut off his oxygen.

She poked his shoulder. "Now move your ass. I need a shower."

When she stood, he placed light, gentle kisses up her body and then pulled her into a hug. "I love you, too."

They walked to the bathroom together. "Are you ready to talk?"

"No."

"I won't freak out. I know your job is dangerous, but I trust you to do everything you can to make it back to me."

She made it easy to want to open up, to let her all the way in. "Did you watch the whole news report?"

"Yeah."

She started the shower. "You coming in?"

He shook his head. "As much as I'd like to, it's probably better if I don't. I'll wash up out here."

"Too bad. I really like it when you get all forceful and take me from behind." She let out a long sigh as she stepped under the water. "Even though I'm in here, I'm still good at listening. You haven't said anything about the fire. I saw the news. I know two kids died."

He took a deep breath and washed up at the sink. Staring down at the running water, he said, "The apartment fire was stubborn. Faulty wiring and too few smoke detectors. We had so many people to evacuate."

He swallowed past the rock in his throat, thinking about the young mother who had been screaming from the curb. "By the time we found them, they weren't breathing. Covered in soot. They were so little."

He closed his eyes against the images of the tiny bodies. His heart crashed in his chest and climbed toward his throat, strangling him. Behind him, the water turned off. He left the room before Evelyn could see what a mess he was.

Unfortunately, she knew him well. She followed, still dripping from her shower. Back in the bedroom, he'd stepped into a pair of underwear and kept his back to her as he gulped air.

She touched his back again in gentle caresses. "What can I do?"

Nothing. No one could do anything. There was no bringing those kids back.

When he didn't turn around, she stepped in front of him. She stroked his jaw and then pulled him close in a tight hug. Burying his face in her neck was a comfort. Emotions rushed out and tears that he hated fell.

Evelyn said nothing. She held him, let him feel in a way he hadn't with another person in years. The anger of not being able to save those kids, the frustration of not being in control, clawed at him. He hated feeling weak.

Everything he kept inside poured from him and she took it, offering comfort in return. With Evelyn, he didn't have to be strong. She allowed him to be vulnerable, which was scarier than any fire he'd ever faced. He'd thought fucking his way through the adrenaline would be enough. He'd convinced himself it was.

Evelyn knew better. She knew him too well. Her pushy nature brought out every ugly, undesirable emotion he had.

But in her arms, he could handle them. Letting them out freed so much in him.

After a few minutes, he was able to breathe easily again, and he stepped away. "I hate that you have the ability to do that to me."

"What?" she whispered.

"Make me fall apart."

She shook her head. "Everyone needs to fall apart sometimes. It's important to have someone who can help put you back together."

They stared at each other, and an entire wordless conversation passed between them.

I'm here for you.

I know.

I love you.

You mean everything to me.

No one could ever be for him what Evelyn was. She smiled as if content with the silent dialogue and said aloud, "I have dinner in the kitchen and a movie picked out if you're up for it."

He returned her smile and surprised himself by saying, "Sure." He was ready for dinner and a movie. Hanging out with his best friend, the woman he loved.

"You go set up the food while I get dressed."

By the time she joined him in the living room, he had dinner on the table. She crawled onto the cushion next to him.

"You okay?"

"I'm gonna be sore tomorrow, but it's going to be the

best kind of sore. Way better than overdoing it on the treadmill."

He laughed. "At least I'm better than a piece of exercise equipment."

"So much better," she said, snuggling close. "Every time I move tomorrow, I'm going to be thinking of you and how long I'll have to wait to get back to bed with you."

Owen smiled. "Any time you want me."

She handed him the remote. He put his arm around her. He was pretty sure he'd found the perfect woman.

OWEN PULLED INTO THE PARKING LOT OF THE BUILDING that Evelyn said was the TV studio, but it looked like any other brick warehouse in the South Loop. He texted to let her know he was there, and she said to come straight in. He hadn't seen her as happy as this in years, maybe ever, even with all the crazy extra hours she had been putting in. So when she'd talked about setting up and running through practice interviews, he had to ask if he could stop by. He wanted to see her in action.

She greeted him at the door and guided him through a maze of hallways to the set. People turned to stare at him as he followed her, but she didn't stop. When they reached the control room, she said, "This is where it all happens."

He looked through the glass and pointed. "Technically, it happens out there, doesn't it?"

"Smart-ass. Without us, nothing good would happen out there."

A woman at the control board snickered.

Evelyn put a hand on the woman's shoulder. "Hailey, this is my boyfriend, Owen. He wanted to see where I work."

Hailey spun in her chair and stuck out her hand. "Nice to meet you."

"And this is Rashid," she said, pointing to the man sitting beside Hailey. "Alaina is usually in here, too, but she's sick."

Owen waved. "Nice to meet you."

The man nodded.

After scooping her hair into a ponytail, Evelyn slipped a headset on. Owen moved to the corner of the room and leaned against the wall.

She spoke into her headset. "Ready, Marilyn?"

On set, Marilyn gave her a thumbs-up.

Evelyn pressed a button and said, "Okay, Danny. Do your thing."

"Who's Danny?" he asked from his post at the wall. Covering her mic, she answered, "My new director. I want to see how he runs things."

Owen crossed his arms and watched. It was weird to see this side of things. He'd visited Evelyn on the set of *Trent Talks*, but she'd put him in the audience and then back in her office when the show was done. She'd never brought him into her space like this before. It really was like watching magic, seeing all the moving parts you're completely unaware of when you watch TV.

After a few minutes, Evelyn said, "Danny, have camera two pan right."

Everyone followed directions, but Evelyn was shaking her head. With her hand over the mic again, she tapped Hailey's shoulder. "Was he this off his game yesterday?"

Hailey nodded.

"Fuck," Evelyn mumbled.

Owen smiled at hearing that she really did drop f-bombs at work. He tried to see what they saw, his attention flipping from the set through the glass to how it appeared on the monitors overhead. It looked like a talk show. A break on set sent people in motion again, moving furniture and refilling glasses of water. Evelyn stiffened and then smiled.

Into her headset, she said, "Yes." She slid a glance to him. "I'd like to know who said that." Then a chuckle. "I'll ask."

She turned to him. "People down on the set, specifically Marilyn, want you to come down and play on camera. She wants to interview you."

Owen shook his head. "I don't want to be on TV."

She stepped closer and lightly touched his hip. "Come on. It'll be fun. We're not actually airing this." Before he had the chance to answer, she spoke into her headset again. "Send Gail up to take him to make up and then to set."

"Makeup? If this isn't being aired, why the hell do I need makeup?"

"This is dress rehearsal. Everything has to be as it should." She took his arm and turned him back to the hallway. "Trust me," she whispered.

He did trust her, but this was all a little too suspicious. A moment later, Gail, a young woman who looked barely out of high school, smiled up at him and said, "This way."

Then there was a blur of activity around him. People put muck all over his face and before he knew it, he was being pushed into a chair beside Marilyn.

He reached across to shake her hand. "It's good to see you again."

"I'm so glad you're here. Maybe when we wrap, we can talk for a bit about some ideas I have for your youth center."

If pretending to be important enough to be on TV would get the center a top-notch fund-raiser, he'd sit there and be interviewed. The lights were sweltering, so he thought the makeup might melt off his face. Some guy neared, adjusted his mic, and then another asked, "Are we ready?"

Owen assumed he was Danny, since he stood near the cameras and began pointing.

"And we're back," Marilyn said. "Joining me now is Owen Hanson, one of Chicago's own firefighters."

He smiled and nodded.

"How long have you been a firefighter, Owen?"

"Almost twenty-two years."

"No other career for you before that?"

"Not unless you count slinging burgers as a teenager. All I ever wanted was to be a firefighter." If all she kept asking about was his job, this would be simple.

"But in addition to saving lives, you also spend quite a bit of your free time volunteering at a youth center, isn't that right?"

He cleared his throat. "Yes. The Chicago Avenue

Youth Center has been an important part of my adult life."

"How did you get started volunteering there?"

"About a decade ago, Sandra, the center's director, put in a request for firefighters to come to the center to talk about fire safety. As soon as I walked in, I fell in love with the place. It's kind of like a beloved neighborhood hangout. It's rough around the edges and needs some TLC, but it gives kids a safe place to be."

"What kinds of activities are offered?"

"Sports—basketball, volleyball—and there's an art class and a homework help room. We also have a lounge where the kids can play video games or listen to music."

"What impact does a place like the center have on the children in the neighborhood?"

"It's more than just the kids. It's the whole neighborhood. Parents know that their kids have a safe place to go. The kids make friends and learn things. Community members love to come in and talk to the kids about different jobs. Some offer internships."

"It sounds like an amazing place."

"It is."

"If you had one wish for the Chicago Avenue Youth Center, what would it be?"

"That's easy—that it would have enough continuous funding to keep the doors open. We don't need fancy technology or new construction. We just need to be there for the families."

"That doesn't seem like you're asking for too much." Marilyn turned to face the cameras. "I challenge all of our viewers to take the money they would spend on one cup of coffee for one day this week and do something better with it. Donate to the Chicago Avenue Youth Center. One cup of coffee. It's that easy to make a difference."

"Cut!" Danny yelled.

Owen leaned over toward Marilyn. "Did you guys have this planned?"

She smirked.

"Can Evelyn hear me?"

Marilyn nodded.

He looked in the general direction of the control booth, even though he couldn't see her. "I'm one lucky son of a bitch. Even when you say you can't do something, you make it happen anyway."

"She's good like that," Marilyn said.

"Yeah, she is."

WHILE AT THE STUDIO A FEW DAYS LATER, EVELYN HEARD mumbling rumors. Something was going on. She tried to eavesdrop because she didn't know any of her crew well enough to just ask. She was their boss, and if it was something they thought would ruffle her, they wouldn't say. After a full day of attempting to listen, she sat in her office with the TV on while she scrolled through headlines on her phone.

That's when she saw the first mention. It was small but noticeable. The nighttime show that Donald was producing had come into question. More specifically, the host and a few of the guests. The story was barely that—only a short paragraph questioning the background of the interviewer. Crap.

Nothing on TV yet, so that was good. Evelyn Googled everything from the name of the show and host to Donald's name to get more information. Nothing. Maybe it was one reporter getting a whiff of something but being off base. She considered calling Donald, but if he'd done something unethical, he wouldn't admit it to her. Best to just let it play out.

The set for *Chi-talk Live* was almost done. Marilyn had been prepping for the first episodes. After her "pretend" interview with Owen, which she hoped would be utilized soon, she ran interviews with members of the crew. Evelyn watched closely from the booth. They were becoming a team. In less than a week, they'd be live.

Marcus only planned to be in town for the first week of airing. Then he was going back to New York or L.A. to continue building his empire. She didn't know what Donald's plans were, but she was looking forward to them stepping back.

Her phone vibrated with a text. Marcus wanted to see her. Scooping up the notes she'd been taking, she went to his office and knocked.

"Come in."

She poked her head through the door. "Hey, Marcus. You wanted to see me?"

"Come in and close the door." He gestured to the chair in front of his desk.

The damn closed door still got to her. Years of working with Harry had set her on edge. She sat, gripping the folder in her lap.

Marcus sighed and pushed back from his desk. He studied her a minute, making her stomach churn. Silence was worse than yelling. She swallowed hard.

"Have you heard anything from Donald?"

She hadn't been expecting that. "No. Should I have?"

"Have you seen this?" He turned his computer screen to face her.

It was the same article she'd read.

"A few minutes ago."

He waited as if she should have something else to add. "Do you know anything about this?"

"No," she said firmly. Whatever Donald had gotten himself into, she wanted no part of it.

"Good."

More silence.

"Do you think there is any truth to it?" Evelyn asked.

He folded his hands on his desk. "Unfortunately, I know there is. I know enough people in the industry that I got word yesterday. This"—he pointed at the screen—"is just the tip. It's going to get ugly. He didn't vet the host or double-check his background. It continued with guests. Nothing they presented is as they said."

Crap. Shit. Fuck. Her heart crashed against her ribs. A behind-the-scenes scandal before they even aired would ruin them. She stared at her clenched hands.

"I have one more question for you."

She looked up.

"If I send Donald packing, are you still on board?"

The buzzing in her head made her think she'd misheard. "Are you asking if I would still run Chi-talk if Donald isn't here?"

"Yes."

"Of course. I developed this idea. I don't want to see it die."

"It won't be easy. You'll have to distance yourself from him and the entire situation."

"Not a problem."

"I'll be informing him soon. When reporters come asking, you know nothing. Keep your head down and get this show running."

She breathed a sigh of relief. She stood to shake his hand. "Thank you."

"This show has too much potential. I'm not going to let poor judgment on Donald's part destroy that."

"One more thing," she said. "What about the crew? They're already talking. That's what tipped me off to look. I don't think they know anything, but they're hearing rumors. How do you want me to address it?"

"I trust your judgment in the matter."

"Thank you again."

Her heart still raced, but something about Marcus's faith in her made her proud. She didn't need Donald for this show to succeed. She went back to the studio where the crew was wrapping up.

She considered waiting until tomorrow to talk to them, but the news cycle moved fast. By tomorrow this story might be huge. She called everyone toward the set.

As they rounded the stage, she waved them closer. "I know you're all ready to go home, but there's something I need to address."

She waited a beat to make sure she had their attention. Making eye contact with each of them, she continued. "There has been some gossip flying around today."

She made a face. "Yeah, I know. We're in TV. There are always rumors."

That earned her a few chuckles. She paused until the laughter subsided. "Something is happening with one of our executive producers. As many of you know, Donald and I were once married, many years ago. However, I don't have the whole story about what is happening now. In fact, some of you probably have more information than I do.

"The story is still developing, and I don't know what's going to happen. What I do know is that it has nothing to do with us and Chi-talk Live. Marcus has assured me that we are on target. This is the only conversation we'll have on the subject. I expect all of you to conduct yourselves professionally. If someone asks you about the situation or about Donald, say nothing."

She inhaled deeply and gave it a moment to sink in. When the crowd began to get restless, she clapped her hands. "That's it. Go home. See you all tomorrow."

They broke and murmured to each other. Evelyn trusted that they would keep their mouths shut. She went back to her office and focused on planning the first episode. She thought about calling Donald to find out how bad it was going to get, but he wouldn't give her the entire truth, anyway.

Chapter Ten

Owen sprawled on his couch, watching a Cubs game while waiting for Evelyn to come home. Every time he had that thought, he considered asking her to move in. Things between them had been going well. He'd never felt so complete and satisfied with his life. In the sixth inning, she shoved through the door, juggling her laptop bag, an overnight duffel, and two bags containing dinner.

He rose to help. "I told you I would've picked up dinner."

"It was on my way."

He took the plastic bags and her duffel. "You know, you could just leave some things here instead of carrying a bag all the time."

"I don't mind." She set her laptop bag next to the couch.

He didn't know how to read that. She didn't mind hauling a bag because she wasn't ready to leave stuff here, or she didn't want to encroach on his space?

"I have space in my closet. Or I can clear out a couple drawers in the dresser." He moved to pull food from the bags, not wanting to reveal that his question was important.

The weight of her stare poked him, and when he looked up, she stood with her head tilted, studying him. "What's going on?" she asked.

"You're hauling a lot of crap back and forth all the time. Just saying that it would be easier if you had some here, that's all."

"Are you sure?"

"Why wouldn't I be? You spend more nights here than we do at your place." It was there, the perfect setup for asking her, but the words wouldn't come.

She stepped close and touched his chest in that way that was uniquely Evelyn. She pressed her lips to his. "If you're sure, I would be happy to keep some clothes here."

His heart lightened. Tugging her onto the couch, he asked, "How was work?"

"Crazy. Something is going on with Donald."

He bit back a snarl and waited.

"There's a story brewing about the show he's producing. Something about the host and guests not being vetted, making up background information. I haven't been able to get the full story yet, but it's not good."

"I'd like to say I'm surprised, but I'm not. The dude is a vulture. All he cares about is ratings."

She opened a container of pasta and took a bite.

"Does this have an effect on your show?"

"Not yet. Marcus called me into his office today to

make sure I would still be on board if he got rid of Donald."

He did a mental fist pump, but kept his calm and said, "You said yes, right?"

"Of course. It wasn't like I wanted to work with Donald again. It was just a by-product of his connection to Marcus." She slid him a smirk. "I bet you're happy."

"I'm not gonna lie. I am happy to know his hands will be off you and your show." He helped himself to a bite of her pasta as he opened his box of chicken Parmesan.

"His hands may have been on my show, but not on me."

"Yeah, they were. Every time he's around, he thinks it's okay to touch you and insert himself in your life. Like because he was your husband years ago, he still has some vested interest."

"I don't see it that way. We're friends. Friends offer advice and support. That's what he's done. Including introducing me to Marcus."

He swallowed and pointed at her with his fork. "Don't you think there was some level of selfishness there? He made the introduction as a means to get his hands on your idea, your show."

He watched as her face went from furrowed brow, ready to argue to a softer look of consideration. She waved her own fork at him. "That might be the case, but you just validated my argument that it had nothing to do with me. Or getting his hands on me. Just my show."

Without another argument, he let the conversation slide. He would probably never be okay with Donald being in her life, but it was enough to know that for now he was gone.

"Do you mind if I change the channel? I want to see if anyone else has picked up the story. Earlier today I could only find a minuscule thing online, but Marcus said it's going to blow up."

He handed her the remote. "If Marcus knew this was happening, why did he let Donald be part of your show?"

She shook her head. "He didn't know until yesterday when someone informed him. He knew before I did and verified the information. When I left the studio, he still didn't know exactly how bad it was going to get, though."

She flipped past local news and went to the national channels, intently reading the scrolling feed at the bottom of the screen. They finished their dinner in relative silence while she stared at the TV. Suddenly, she jumped up. "This is it."

There was a brief note at the bottom of the screen. He didn't know what she was talking about.

"Nighttime Investigations with Charlie Varner. That's the name of the show Donald's been working on." She waited a beat. "No mention of Donald. He might escape this yet."

"Where's my phone?" Owen asked. "There's got to be a tip line somewhere. I can make sure he doesn't escape."

She laughed as she leaned back into the couch. "We need to keep as far from this as possible. I don't want any stink rubbing off on me."

"Spoilsport."

She returned the remote to him so he could choose a show. She turned her attention to her phone and read more headlines. He sighed. A distracted Evelyn was still better than Evelyn tied to Donald.

Then the damn thing rang. From his position next to her, he saw that it was Donald. Her finger hovered over the answer button.

"Don't do it. You said you needed to keep your distance."

"I was talking about the news and publicity." Another two rings. Then she answered. "Hello."

Damn it. He hated that she always responded to Donald. No matter what.

"EVIE. I ASSUME YOU'VE HEARD."

"I've seen a couple of headlines and listened to some rumors. What the hell happened?"

"It's TV. You know how it goes. People lie."

She shifted away from Owen, who was giving her dagger eyes. What was she supposed to do? Ignore Donald? He'd just call again. Plus, this way, she could get the real story to protect herself and the show.

"It's your job as a producer to weed through the lies."

He chuffed. "Like you've never had anyone pull one over on you?"

Only you. But she bit back that response.

"I'm sure I have. But I've always done due diligence to vet every guest. From the little bit I've read, you didn't even vet your host. You touted him as this hardened journalist who reported from the front lines and across the globe. He's never left the damn country." The more she thought about it, the more her anger rose. It had been sloppy.

"Come on. Why would I think he would lie about something like that? Everyone who's ever worked with him told the same stories. It wasn't just me that he fooled."

He had a point, but it didn't matter.

"You're the one paying for it, though. It wouldn't have happened if you'd done a better job. Letting in a fraud allowed him the opportunity to run with fraudulent stories. How much of what you aired was fabricated?"

"Who knows? At this point, I'm afraid to look. It might be as much as half. Made for good viewing at least."

"If it was being sold as fiction, you'd be fine. This was supposed to be news." She thought about bringing up Marcus but decided to wait. Marcus had said he would talk to Donald, but she didn't know if it had happened yet. Another thing she wanted to keep away from her.

"I'm at the airport on my way back to Chicago."

Damn. Well, that answered whether Marcus had talked to him. "That's probably not a good idea."

"I need to talk to Marcus. That's not a phone conversation. I'll see you tomorrow."

"Okay." She disconnected and leaned on Owen again, who was pretending to watch baseball.

"Did you make Donald feel better?" he sneered.

"I wanted to find out how bad it's going to get. From the little bit Donald admitted to, it'll be big. He thinks half of the stories he aired as news were fabricated."

She was unsettled, even though she loved being snuggled next to Owen. Something about Donald's lack of care in regard to his work bothered her. He'd taught her so much about producing and how to run a good show, she couldn't believe he'd been so lackadaisical. While the boring baseball game droned on, her mind raced.

She began to wonder how far-reaching an investigation into Donald's work would be. She shouldn't worry, because she knew all the work she'd done with him had been vetted. Her heart rate picked up. At least that's how she remembered it. She'd been in love with him. He easily could have lied about checking into someone or something and she would've believed him.

Back on her phone, she dug deeper for headlines and articles. She wanted to find the names of people on the hunt.

Owen kissed the top of her head. "What are you doing now?"

"I just had this horrible worry about people questioning the work I did with Donald."

"You would never do anything unethical."

"Not intentionally. But back then... If Donald had told me to run with something, I would have." Her gut twisted with the admission.

He muted the TV. "Why would anyone go back that far if they've got him dead to rights for what he's doing now?"

"To seal his fate?" she answered with a shrug. "I need

to figure out who's running with the story. If it's someone with an ax to grind, they'll go back. I know I would."

"Anything I can do to help?"

"No. I just need to check into this more."

"I guess Donald wasn't forthcoming, huh?"

"He admitted he didn't vet his host. But the guy and his phony background were accepted by others in the business. That's what's making me worry about who's doing this."

"So you need to find who Donald pissed off." He chuckled. "That'll be a long list."

She poked him in his side. "Believe it or not, most people generally like Donald."

"I don't believe it."

He twisted to face her, pushing her back against the opposite side of the couch. "You're spending too much time thinking about this." He lowered his mouth to hers. "Your job is secure. Donald is out of the picture. If the shit hits the fan, it has nothing to do with you."

"But—" Her words were lost when his tongue made contact with the side of her neck.

He took his time nibbling and sucking and driving her mad with his mouth. She dropped her phone, and it thumped on the floor.

She held Owen close, luxuriating in the safety and security he offered.

EVELYN WOKE WITH A START, HER PHONE BUZZING crazily on the bedside table. Brushing her hair off her face, she picked it up and looked at the screen. A slew of texts from various people she knew in TV, some of whom were currently on her crew. Something had broken overnight in regard to Donald. She looked over her shoulder. Owen was already up.

She heard the shower running, so she went to the kitchen. He always started the coffee before heading to the shower. It was one of the many things she could count on with him. With a huge steaming cup in front of her, she focused on the messages. Most were in the vein of *Did you see about Donald? I can't believe it!* When she scrolled through, she found what she'd been looking for: links. She opened one after another.

It was far worse than Donald had led her to believe. They not only had a fraud for a host but the stories he'd said were fabricated weren't actually made-up. They just belonged to someone else. They'd interviewed people who had amazing stories, then had decided to embellish them and brought in other people who'd acted as though the stories were theirs.

Owen came into the kitchen. "What's up?"

"Shit hit the fan overnight."

He picked up her cup and drank. "Everything still okay for you?"

"I think so." She rose, kissed his cheek, and said, "I'm going into the studio now to make sure. See you tomorrow?"

He put the cup back on the table and grabbed her hips. "As soon as I'm off shift. I'll wake you up." He kissed her, showing a hint of what he'd do to wake her.

"I have to go. Have a good day at work."

"You, too."

As she drove to the studio, Evelyn considered how lucky she was to have Owen. She'd thought his weird work schedule would bother her, but it worked well for them. He didn't nag her about the time she spent at work, and she didn't get mopey when she didn't see him for more than twenty-four hours. She really liked that he had nothing to do with TV.

When she had started dating Donald and for their entire marriage, there was no break or escape. They'd had so much in common, they'd understood the struggles and disappointments. But because they'd worked together, she'd never had someone to vent to or share stories with. She believed that was part of the downfall of their marriage. When she'd needed to vent about work, Donald had told her how to play it, what to do, instead of just listening. He'd acted as if she couldn't handle her own problems.

Owen, on the other hand, assumed she could manage anything. She could vent and he didn't offer unsolicited advice, especially about things he didn't understand. She'd definitely traded up. She pulled into the lot and saw a few cameras out front. Hopefully, no one knew who she was and they'd just come looking for Donald. She left her car and walked quickly to a back entrance. When she neared her office, everyone was buzzing. She hadn't heard from Marcus, and she didn't know if that was a positive sign. Donald was in Chicago, possibly in this building. She sat at her desk and tried to bury her nose in work, but it was useless.

As soon as she had her computer booted up, she

began to track the story on Donald's mess. She'd barely gotten through the first story when there was a knock on her door. She looked up to see Donald standing there.

"Hey, Evie."

"Hey."

"I have a favor to ask."

Damn. She really couldn't afford to get involved in this.

He came into the office and closed the door. "I need to stay at your place for a few days."

"What?"

"I already had people showing up at my home before I left New York. That was before things went crazy. Now, in case you haven't noticed, they're outside."

"I noticed. I was praying they don't know who I am."

He smiled that I'm-so-charming grin that worked on everyone. "Come on. It's not that bad being my ex."

She snorted. "Right now, it's the worst position to be in."

He dropped the smile and sighed. "They'll follow me to my hotel. I just need to lie low for a couple of days. They'll forget all about me when the news cycle shifts."

She crossed her arms. "I don't know. This is pretty big."

"Evie, I'm sure Marcus told you that he's cut my involvement here. Isn't that enough punishment? You get to go on and have this amazing new show, and I have to find something to salvage my career."

She had a feeling that he'd be just fine. But guilt still tugged at her. He made valid points. This deal might not exist with Marcus if Donald hadn't made the introductions. He always had her back and did what he could to advance her career. She bit her lip. What was a few days? She'd just stay with Owen.

"Fine. I expect you to keep my place clean and replace anything you eat." She rolled her chair over to the corner where she dropped her bag. Pulling out her keys, she separated the ones for Owen's house and tossed the rest to Donald. "My car is in the back lot. Fill the tank."

"You're not coming with me?"

"Why would I? I still have a job, remember?" she said with a smirk.

"That was a cheap shot. You trust me in your house alone? Imagine the trouble I can get into."

She waved a hand. "Whatever. Stay out of my personal stuff. Sleep in the guest room."

He tossed the keys in the air and caught them. "You're taking away the little bit of fun I should be able to have."

"Do not include me in the fun you think you should have." It was bad enough that he'd made these egregious mistakes—assuming they were actually mistakes, because with Donald she never knew—and would probably get away with barely a mark against him. She tried not to be bitter about what men could get away with. If she'd done half of what Donald had done or at least allowed others to do, she'd never work in TV again.

Donald winked. "We always had fun."

"Had. Past tense."

He sighed again. "Yeah, I know. You're with Owen. I still don't quite understand the compatibility there."

I have a man who doesn't put work before our relation-

ship. Someone who gives me comfort and stability, who balances my life. A man who doesn't manipulate every aspect of our lives to further his wants. A man who treats me like I'm a goddess.

"Good thing you don't need to understand. Now get out. I have work to do."

"Okay. See you later." He turned to leave and then spun around. "Thank you."

"No problem. It's only a couple of days, right?"

"Absolutely. Maybe you can invite Owen over, and we can all have dinner together."

She laughed again. "I sincerely doubt that's a good idea. In case you haven't noticed, he doesn't like you."

"I don't know why. I'm a fascinating person."

She pursed her lips and pointed at the door again. This time when he turned, he continued walking.

With Donald out of the picture and the reassurance that her job was safe, she focused on prepping for their first episode. They planned on having a run-through in a few days. Marcus was pushing because the network had an open slot and he wanted them to fill it. The excitement for her project returned full force. She was determined to make this a hit.

OWEN LEFT THE FIREHOUSE AND DROVE HOME ON autopilot. When he didn't see Evelyn's car, he tried to remember if she'd said she was staying at her place and he should come there. His only thought had been crawling into bed with her and making love until she had to leave for work. He drove to her place and parked.

On his way upstairs, he began to imagine the different ways he could subtly wake her. He briefly wondered if he could get his face between her legs to lick her pussy. He unlocked the door and tossed his keys on the counter.

As he reached for the hem of his T-shirt to pull it over his head, he heard a noise and stopped. From around the corner, Donald strode into the room wearing nothing but a towel.

"What the fuck!"

Donald froze, eyes wide.

A lifetime passed with the two of them staring at each other. Water dripped down Donald's chest, and Owen saw red. Images flashed in his mind of Evelyn naked in bed with this asshole, running her tongue over his chest, doing all the things she should only be doing with him. He stormed forward.

Donald gripped the knot in his towel with one hand and raised the other. "It's not what you think."

"Right." His fist snapped back before he considered what he was doing, and then he connected with Donald's jaw. The man slipped in his bare feet and lost the hold he had on his towel. Owen sniffed as he stepped over Donald. "Evelyn!"

He didn't know why he was calling her. Did he want to see the evidence of what she'd been doing with her ex?

Flinging the towel back in place, Donald pushed off the floor. "She's not here. That's what I tried to tell you."

"I didn't ask you," Owen growled. He turned, and Donald flinched as he walked past.

Disgust filled Owen's gut. He knew. As soon as Donald swooped back into her life, he knew the man couldn't be trusted. He would do whatever he could to keep a toehold in Evelyn's life. Donald continued to stammer something, but Owen was deaf. His blood thundered in his ears, and he stormed out of the condo.

This time when he drove home, it wasn't just on autopilot. He was in a blind rage. It wasn't the wisest choice, but there was no way he could sit in his car outside Evelyn's and think about Donald's naked ass.

He parked in front of his house and had no recollection of how he'd gotten there. Inside, he absently patted Probie's head. In the kitchen, he found a note from Evelyn.

Sorry I missed you. Call when you wake up.

As if he had any chance of sleeping now. His heart was still pounding. He wanted to hit something. Preferably Donald again. He changed into running clothes and grabbed Probie's leash. His dog danced around his legs the way he always did.

They ran hard. Owen didn't even track how far they'd gone. It hadn't been a relaxing, stay-fit kind of run. He just kept running, driving pictures from his imagination. Images of a naked Donald standing in Evelyn's living room. By the time he rounded the corner near his house, poor Probie was panting and slowing down. That was how he knew they'd gone farther than ever. His dog never tired.

He opened the door and went straight to the kitchen to get fresh cold water. While Probie lapped at his bowl, Owen gulped from a glass. His body radiated heat from the run and his anger, which hadn't waned at all. He looked at his phone and saw missed calls from Evelyn. He turned the phone off.

There was nothing to say. It didn't matter what was going on at her place. Donald should never have been there, comfortable enough to strip down and take a shower. He didn't care how many times Evelyn said they were friends. He knew exactly how that played out. Evelyn had told him that for months after their separation and divorce, she'd hopped into bed with Donald. Then, of course, there was Stacy and her special friend.

His thoughts sat like acid in his brain. It was still morning, but he really wanted to open a beer. However, drinking wouldn't solve anything. He considered calling his brother or maybe Trevor, but he didn't want advice. He took a quick shower and lay down to sleep. Anything to erase the betrayal he saw in his mind.

Chapter Eleven

Evelyn couldn't focus on a damn thing after she received the call from Donald. She knew what Owen thought, especially after finding Donald at her house, taking a shower. Part of her was pissed that he would even think she would cheat on him. But mostly, she was worried. Owen would be a mess.

She'd called his phone so many times, she was getting desperate. She wanted to leave work, but since they were getting their first episode ready, she couldn't afford to take off in the middle of the day. There was still too much to do.

Between trying to fill audience seats for an unknown show to fielding ridiculous questions about Donald, she was barely keeping her head above water. And Owen's actions were pulling her under. She left him a message, but knowing him, he wouldn't even listen to it. If, by chance, he did listen, it still probably wouldn't do much good. He was a stubborn man. She put her head down and got to work, even though she constantly checked her phone on the off chance that he might call.

Later that night—always later than she thought she'd be leaving work—she called him again. Straight to voicemail. So after grabbing a ride to her place to pick up her car, she drove to his house to make him listen to reason.

The house was dark, but his car was out front, so he was home. She pulled out her keys and considered walking in, but then decided to knock. He was mad. He wouldn't want her barging in.

No answer. She knocked harder. Probie barked, and she heard the dog scrambling on the other side of the door. Maybe he'd gone out?

Then she heard the curse. The door yanked open and he stood in the entryway. His face was indifferent at seeing her. It shouldn't have hurt, but it did.

Shoring up her defense, she said, "Can I come in?"

"Why bother?"

Then she noticed how he swayed. He'd been drinking.

"Are you drunk?"

"Not nearly enough. Couldn't sleep. What do you want? To tell me that it's not what I think? That Donald's naked ass wasn't strolling through your condo?"

"Yes. No." She closed her eyes and took a breath. "Yes, Donald was at my place. I was not. I spent the night here. How could you think I would ever cheat on you, much less with Donald?"

"There are other ways to cheat besides letting some guy put his dick in you."

"What?"

"Go home, Evelyn." He moved to close the door.

She slapped her palm against it. "No. You don't get to say shit and then brush me off like I don't matter."

"You don't. You made your choice. And it wasn't me."

His first words more than stung. A stabbing pain thrust through her. Then the rest of his statement registered. "What the hell are you talking about?"

"He's staying at your place, Evelyn. He doesn't fucking belong there."

"His life is imploding. His career is in question, he just lost the job with my show, and reporters are all over his place. I'm helping a friend."

He growled.

"That's all he is, Owen."

He shook his head and gave her a look of disgust. "You choose him. All. The. Time. Phone rings. It's Donald. Let me take this. Donald shows up in town. I'm going out to dinner with Donald. Donald fucked up his life. Let me help." With each phrase his volume increased and his arms waved for emphasis. It was the most non-Owen-like she'd ever seen him.

She took another deep breath. "Can I come in so we can talk?"

"There's nothing to talk about. Your priorities are clear. And I'm not one."

For fuck's sake. "You're drunk. Call me when you're ready to have a conversation." She turned and left. The problem was, she didn't know where she was supposed to go. Donald was still at her place, and he was the last person she wanted to see right now. As she drove through the city, anger bit at her. Men were so stupid. She called Nina.

"Hey, what's up?"

"Are you at home?" she asked.

"Yeah."

"Can I come over? I need a place to stay tonight."

"What's going on?"

"I'll explain when I get there. Have the wine ready."

When Evelyn arrived at Nina's apartment, which was bigger than Evelyn's condo, Nina already had wine poured for both of them.

"Tell me," Nina said.

"This is all your fault." She accepted the glass, settled on the couch, and then told her friend what happened.

"How is any of that my fault?"

"You and your stupid challenge for us to find someone to be with. Specifically calling out me and Owen for our relationship. That was all you. We were fine."

"Were you?" Nina's question was full of innuendo.

They had been fine. Their lives had been good. Admittedly, they were better now. At least until today. It was all jumbled up.

"So Owen thinks you slept with Donald?"

Evelyn shrugged. "I have no clue what Owen thinks. He's mad. He's drunk. He thinks I chose Donald over him." She glugged more wine.

"As if."

"Right? How could he think I would ever do anything like that?"

Waving her glass at Evelyn, Nina said, "He did find a naked Donald in your living room."

"First, he wasn't really naked. He had a towel on because he'd just gotten out of the shower. Second, he was only in the living room because he heard Owen come in. Owen jumped to all kinds of conclusions."

Nina raised her eyebrows. "Still…"

"Still, what?" Where was Nina going with this? She couldn't be siding with Owen.

"How would you react if a naked chick was at Owen's place?"

Evelyn stopped and thought for a minute. She couldn't imagine it. Over the years, she'd been there when a woman had spent the night, but she'd never walked in on anything. But now? She knew he would never do that. "I would be shocked, but I'd also give him the benefit of the doubt."

"I don't know that Owen can do that in this type of situation. His wife cheated on him. For all the group counseling and healing he's done, I don't know that he's truly gotten past it." She sipped from her glass. "He has trust issues."

"We all have trust issues. You decide what's important and take a chance."

"He did. He took a chance on you, and now he has doubts."

She listened. She knew Nina spoke the truth. It was nothing she didn't already know about Owen, but she was still angry that he doubted her. Sadness fought the anger. "I didn't do anything wrong."

She gulped her wine, hoping to drown all of the feelings. Tomorrow would look better. Owen would sober up and in the light of day, he'd realize how ridiculous this was.

"I'm not accusing you of doing anything wrong. I'm just saying that maybe you should cut Owen some slack."

The sadness won over the anger. "But how could he even think I would sleep with Donald?"

"I don't know. I thought if anyone would get him to move on it would be you. He's always loved you."

They sat in silence, drinking wine. Nina made some dinner, but to Evelyn it was tasteless. Thoughts of Owen filled her head. She didn't know how to convince him of how much she loved him, that she would never cheat on him.

SHE HAD A RESTLESS NIGHT IN NINA'S GUEST ROOM before going home. She needed to change to get ready for work. When she shoved the door to the condo open, she called, "Donald?"

It was early, but Donald had always been an early riser. He came around the corner. At least he was fully dressed.

"Hey, Evie. Everything okay?"

"No. Nothing is okay. You need to go."

"What? You said I could stay for a few days."

"That was before you cost me my relationship with Owen."

"What are you talking about? I told him he was misreading the situation." He straightened his tie and picked up a cup of coffee. Totally comfortable in her space.

That's when it hit her. Owen had been right. She let Donald stroll into her life whenever he wanted. And although she didn't sleep with him, he was here. In her place.

"Letting you stay here was a mistake. Owen doesn't particularly like you, and he definitely doesn't trust you. I should've paid more attention to that before agreeing to let you stay."

"Come on, Evie. It's just a couple of days."

She clenched her jaw and inhaled sharply through her nose. "Do not call me Evie. I'm not a child. You made a mess of your life, and you can't use me to hide out."

"After all I've done for you?"

She crossed her arms with an eye roll. "I'll admit that you helped me early in my career. But I've built what I have. I'm a respected producer. I stepped out of your shadow a long time ago."

"Did you forget I brokered the deal with Marcus?"

She snorted. "Why exactly did you do that? Was it because you believed in me and my show or was it your way of getting your hands on my idea?"

"That's a hell of a way to thank me."

"I thanked you for the introduction to Marcus. You have no right to anything else."

"That's the way it's going to be?"

She walked over to the door and held it open. "It's the way it has to be. I've moved on with my life. You need to do the same."

He disappeared into the bedroom and returned a

few minutes later wheeling his suitcase behind him. She stepped into the hallway to let him pass.

"Good luck," she said.

He leaned in to kiss her, and she swayed back. With a shove to his shoulder, she pointed to the elevator. "No more."

He smiled and shook his head. "Had to give it a shot. I'll call when things settle down."

"Don't. We both need space." She went inside, poured herself coffee, and stripped the bed to remove any sign that Donald had been there. For the first time in her life, she'd thrown Donald out and stood her ground. It was an accomplishment. And the one person she always wanted to share her accomplishments with wouldn't take her calls.

She stepped into the shower. That was where tears finally fell. Fear that Owen wouldn't realize he had overreacted overwhelmed her. She loved him and didn't want to lose him.

As she finished her coffee, she stared at her phone. One more time. She'd call and leave him a message.

"Hi. I know you're mad. I want to talk. I threw Donald out. I get it now. Please call me back." If he didn't return her call, she'd go talk to him again.

Then she left her house and went to work. She had a show to put on.

OWEN HAD STOPPED DRINKING IN PLENTY OF TIME TO BE sober and functioning at work. But he still felt like shit. He'd finally turned his phone off to avoid hearing from Evelyn. He had nothing to say to her. When he turned it back on, not only did he have calls from her to ignore, he had two from Nina, one from Trevor, and even one from Gabe. If anyone could understand where he was coming from, it would be Gabe.

Gabe had told them all for as long as they'd known him that no one could really be trusted. Maybe he should go live like Gabe. Cut everyone out and be alone. He stood outside the firehouse and called his friend.

"Yes?"

"You called but didn't leave a message."

Gabe sighed. "Nina called me. Said that you and Evelyn are fighting."

"Not fighting. To fight, you have to care. I'm done."

"Bullshit."

"What?"

"Tell that lie to someone who might believe it. You're pissed because her ex is hanging on. I get it. But you know Evelyn. She knows your history. She wouldn't sleep with him."

He bit back a curse. The one friend who he thought would back him wasn't being helpful. "Look, I just got to work. I wanted to make sure whatever you called for wasn't important. It obviously wasn't."

"See you for coffee in the morning?"

"Is Evelyn going to be there?"

"No idea."

"Then probably not."

Gabe mumbled something that resembled a curse. They disconnected.

He'd barely been at work long enough to settle in when Jamal yelled from the front, "Hey, Owen. You have a guest."

"What?" No one ever came to the firehouse.

Standing in the doorway of the bay was Evelyn. Sun shining on her brown hair hinting at red tones. His heart lurched. He wanted nothing more than to go to her and pull her into his arms.

Stupid fucking heart.

Tucking his hands into his pockets, he asked, "What are you doing here?"

She smiled. "Since you won't call me back and you can't close a door in my face here, I figured we could talk."

"I'm working."

She tilted her head as if to listen. "No alarms are ringing. I think you can spare a few minutes."

"There's nothing to say."

"I have something to say."

He crossed his arms and waited.

She stepped closer, raised a hand as if to touch him, but then dropped it. "First, I didn't sleep with Donald. I am absolutely not interested in him. Second, I love you. I would never do anything to intentionally hurt you."

He sniffed in disbelief.

A flash of irritation crossed her face. "I made a poor choice. Donald asked to stay at my place, and I didn't consider how that would make you feel. I'm sorry for that. I was at your house, so I didn't think about it at all.

But I should have. When I went back home, I told Donald to leave."

The idea that after he turned her away she went back to Donald still rubbed him wrong. It shouldn't matter. He was done, right?

"In telling him to leave, I realized a few things. I do let Donald have too much space in my life. I don't know why I've done that. A lot of shared time and history. The power he holds that could impact my career. I never really thought about it. But I should have listened closer to you. For that, I am sorry."

He didn't know what to say. His heart leaped in his chest, screaming at him to accept her apology and kiss her. He swallowed it back down.

"Are you done?"

She nodded. He turned his back and started to walk away.

"Where the hell are you going?"

"Back to work," he said over his shoulder.

"So that's it?" she called. "You overreact, I apologize, and it's still over? You're going to throw away years of friendship for what?"

He spun on his heels. "You threw it away. Tossing around an 'I'm sorry' doesn't change what you did."

Her throat worked as she swallowed. Her eyes filled, but she blinked rapidly. "You're going to be alone forever if you can't accept that people screw up, Owen. We all do. Even you."

She walked away. Her parting words felt truer than he wanted to admit. Watching Evelyn leave felt like the biggest mistake of his life.

As he left work the following morning, his phone buzzed with a text from Gabe.

Meet me at Sunny's in 10. I have something to show you.

He answered.

I just got off work. Going home.

Get your ass here. It's important.

He checked the time. He could make it to the diner in time, which would be earlier than they usually met. It might be possible to find out whatever Gabe wanted to show him and leave before anyone else arrived. He didn't want to listen to advice about his ruined relationship.

He drove to Sunny's and found Gabe at their usual table. His stomach flipped. He and Evelyn came together more often than not. What would his life look like now?

Gabe pushed a cup of coffee in his direction.

"I don't think Evelyn is coming today. First day of her new show."

He sank into the chair and drank the coffee. "I don't want to talk about Evelyn."

"Whatever. I told her you guys were a bad idea."

That took Owen aback. "You did?" He'd been sure everyone in their group had been cheering from the sidelines. Against his better judgment, he asked, "Why?"

He pointed around the table at the empty chairs. "For this exact reason. Our group would explode."

"Maybe it's time we all moved on."

"No." Gabe's emphatic statement was strange for the usually quiet guy. "You might find this hard to believe, but I don't socialize much. You guys have given me the most normalcy I've had since my divorce. I can't afford to lose that."

Owen took another drink of coffee. "So Evelyn and I will take turns coming. I'm not saying we can't be friends."

Gabe looked agitated. As if any alteration in his routine and group of friends was unacceptable.

"She didn't cheat on you."

Owen huffed. "How would you know?"

"Besides the fact that I know Evelyn? Even an idiot like me can see she loves you. But I have proof."

"Huh?" How could anyone prove the lack of anything?

Gabe pulled out his phone. "Security cameras at the studio show Donald leaving at one forty-two. Evelyn continued working that day until after seven, at which point, she went to your house."

"How do you—"

"I hacked the security feed, then pinged her phone. She was nowhere near her condo."

"Until I didn't let her in."

"Wrong again. She spent the night at Nina's." He

swiped the screen on his phone. "And then there's this." He turned it to let Owen see.

On the screen, a grainy video that showed Evelyn's hallway. She stood in the doorway, arms crossed.

"What the hell, Gabe?"

"Don't ask. Just watch."

He returned his focus to the screen. A moment later, Donald came through the door with a suitcase. They spoke and then he leaned in. Owen's jaw clenched. But Evelyn's hand came up to Donald's shoulder and pushed him away. Then she pointed down the hall.

She'd told the truth. She had thrown him out.

Gabe put his phone away. "Donald was on the next flight back to New York. There hasn't been any contact since."

"So she didn't fuck him. She still let him stay at her place. He's always there in her life."

"I can't believe I'm gonna say this, but we all have baggage. History. You can't just pretend it doesn't exist. Your baggage is Stacy. Hers is Donald. The difference is, Stacy did something to make you keep your distance. Evelyn didn't have that experience. But she's hurting now." Gabe drank his coffee. "And that's all on you."

He listened but had no idea what he was supposed to do. Part of him had always believed Evelyn hadn't fucked Donald, but the whole situation still felt wrong. "It's not like you to get all up in anyone's business."

"This business is messing with the balance of my life. I don't like it."

He chuckled. That was more like the Gabe he knew. He didn't want to repair Owen's relationship with

Evelyn because he believed they belonged together. He just didn't like the inconvenience to his life.

He drained his coffee. "Tell everyone I said hi."

"You're not staying? I told you Evelyn's at work."

"First, stop hacking into our lives. Second, I can't listen to them, especially Nina."

Gabe grunted his understanding. Owen tossed a few bills on the table and left. He drove home thinking about Evelyn and everything that had happened. Probie offered his usual happy greeting at the door. He wasn't up for a run. In his bedroom, he looked at the space he'd cleared for Evelyn. It was empty. She must've come by while he was at work and taken her stuff.

The empty drawers stared at him. Then he noticed a pile of his neatly folded clothes. Random T-shirts and shorts that she'd borrowed when she'd spent the night. He'd been kidding about wanting them back, yet here they were. He was back to being alone. More alone than he'd been in years, because now he didn't have Evelyn.

He plopped on the couch, turned on the TV, and waited for Evelyn's show. He watched the full hour. Marilyn interviewed people, but he didn't pay much attention. In his mind's eye, he saw Evelyn in the control room bossing people around, saying an occasional "fuck" when things weren't going as planned.

Just as the show was about over, Marilyn said they had one more segment that they'd taped. She introduced the Chicago Avenue Youth Center. Then they aired the interview he'd done. The one Evelyn had said was practice.

His heart swelled. She'd done that for him. He was such an asshole.

What the fuck have I done?

Chapter Twelve

The first episode aired, and it felt amazing. Evelyn was supercharged like she'd downed four cups of espresso. In truth is was only three cups of regular coffee, but the buzz she felt was more about a job well done.

They'd nailed it. Her phone went crazy as soon as the cameras shut down. Most were texts of congratulations. One was from Marcus.

Come to my office.

He might be pissed that she chose to air Owen's segment. She was willing to face the music on that. But first, a quick celebration with her crew. When she reached the set, everyone broke out in applause. Yeah, they were her crew. This was going to be good.

"Good job, everyone. I ordered pizzas to celebrate." The studio erupted in cheers. "Don't get used to it. Our budget isn't that big. But we started with an idea just a few short weeks ago and we nailed our first episode. You should be proud."

As she turned to leave, Marilyn grabbed her and pulled her into a hug. "Thank you for bringing me in on this. I love it."

"I knew you'd be perfect, and you are. Congratulations."

People around her said kind words and offered congratulations, but inside she was empty. She had no one to celebrate with.

She headed to the elevators to go to Marcus's office. Her phone bleeped again. Owen. Just seeing his name on her screen made her tear up. She swiped to open the message.

> I hope you don't get in trouble for airing that awful interview with me. The center will be grateful. Thank you.

Her heart sank again. The center would be grateful. Not him. She could hear his self-deprecating chuckle talking about how bad the interview was and how he didn't look good on camera. All lies, of course.

So this would be their new normal. Polite conversation.

She didn't think she could do it. But she texted the same answer Marcus would get momentarily.

> We had an open spot and couldn't have dead air. Your interview filled a few needed minutes.

He didn't respond. Bracing to defend herself, she entered Marcus's office. "You wanted to see me?"

"Have a seat." He pointed to the chair in front of him. "Good first show."

"Thank you. I think it went well."

"We're getting a lot of buzz. People are talking."

"Excellent."

"I thought we agreed not to do a segment on the youth center right now."

She took a slow inhale. "I know you didn't think it was a good idea. It was a little unplanned. We taped that during rehearsal with Marilyn. When we prepped Jake Drummer for his interview, he was smooth and polished. You saw him today. We cut his segment short because it was awful. I needed something to fill the space."

"It was a good call."

Wait. What?

"The segment wasn't the downer Donald had expected it to be. And your firefighter friend was really good on camera. Airing it against my call took guts. It affirms my decision to hire you." He stood and stuck out his hand.

She rose without thought and shook his hand. Her new boss had just congratulated her for not following orders. Because she was damn good at her job.

"Thank you. Any recommendations going forward?"

"Keep it up."

She left his office riding a high that was limited by her brief exchange with Owen. In her office, she had a bunch of interviewees to confirm for upcoming shows. They'd have a meeting tomorrow to brainstorm new episodes. Instead of doing any of that, she opened her phone and stared at the text from Owen, trying to read between the lines, willing it to mean something more.

Taking her things from his house had been one of the hardest things she'd ever done. Even harder was leaving a bag of his clothes that she'd borrowed. While he'd joked that she might have had a third of his wardrobe, she definitely had more than she'd let on. Now everything was back to its rightful owners. And everything felt wrong.

After a few hours of slogging through work that she normally breezed through, her phone rang. She answered without looking at the screen. "Hello?"

"Hey," Owen's deep voice rumbled across the line. Her fingers froze on her keyboard. Had it only been a couple of days since she'd heard his voice? It felt like weeks.

"You there, Evelyn?"

"Yeah." Her voice was barely a whisper.

"I'm sorry. I've been a jerk and I should know better."

Her lungs filled with much-needed oxygen. "Yeah, you should have."

"I don't know if I can fix this, but I want to. What I said and how I acted were way out of line."

"Yep."

"The thought of you with anyone else pushes me to a place where I can't think. My reaction was worse. I pushed you away, but I can't function without you in my life."

Tears dripped down her face.

"I love you, Evelyn."

"Why the sudden change?"

He paused. "I talked to Gabe."

"Gabe?" she asked with a laugh. Had he said Trevor or even Nina, it would've made sense. They would've told him he was being an asshole. But Gabe thought them being together was a bad idea. "What did he say?"

"He convinced me that I was wrong."

"How the hell did Gabe of all people convince you?" This should be one hell of a story.

"Don't get mad. He did some unethical stuff, but he did it because he cares about us."

"What do you mean?" Her nerves prickled uneasily.

"He hacked security cameras to show you throwing Donald out."

"What?" Her voice rose and her happy tears quickly dried up.

"I said don't get mad."

"Wait. Are you telling me that Gabe hacked into my life to prove to you that I wasn't cheating on you?" Rage that was becoming all too familiar bubbled up.

"He did it to help fix things. Gabe wasn't thinking—"

"Stop. You're misunderstanding my outrage. Gabe was being Gabe, and believe me when I say I'll make sure he understands how wrong that was. But you...you call me with this apology, telling me you love me, but it's only because you were handed irrefutable proof that I was honest. That's bullshit, Owen. You don't treat someone you love like that."

"That wasn't—"

She didn't wait to hear the rest of his rationalization. She hung up. She had enough of him yanking her emotions around. Even after everything she'd said and done for him, he'd needed Gabe to tell him that she hadn't cheated. She couldn't be with a man who couldn't—or didn't want to trust her. Where had her best friend gone? More tears fell as she accepted that her relationship with Owen was over.

When Evelyn finally dragged herself home that night, she couldn't help but look at her guest parking spot, the one usually occupied by Owen. It had been empty for days, but today someone was parked there. What the hell? It was her spot. She eyed the minivan and recognition hit. It was Tess. As soon as Evelyn stepped from her car, the doors on the minivan popped open and Tess and Nina sprang out.

"Thank God," Nina said. "We've been waiting forever."

"We have not," Tess said.

They both rushed forward carrying grocery bags.

"What's all this?" Evelyn asked, pointing to the bags.

"We figured you needed a girls' night."

"I suggested we go out and get you rip-roaring drunk, but Tess pooh-poohed that idea."

Hearing Nina talk about getting her drunk felt weird because she'd never even seen Nina have more than a glass of wine to be social, much less tie one on. Her family history with alcoholism still hit her hard.

"I'm not up for going out anyway," she said. "With this being the first week of shows, I have to be sharp."

Tess held up her totes. "Hence, the bags. Let's go in

and you can tell us what the hell is going on with you and Owen."

Evelyn swallowed hard. "In a nutshell, we're done."

She turned and led her friends into her condo. Part of her wanted to crawl under the covers and not deal with anyone, but the rest of her was grateful she had good friends who would take care of her. Inside, she kicked off her heels. "I'm going to change. Make yourselves comfortable."

She went to her bedroom and pulled on sweats.

Nina called, "Ice cream or alcohol?"

It had been so long since she had a breakup pity party, she didn't know what to do. *Both* was her initial reaction, but since she didn't want to get sick, she said, "Maybe stick with junk food."

She joined her friends in the living room. Plopping on the couch, she found an assortment of bad choices to drown her sorrows in. When was the last time she'd done this? How had she mended her broken heart last time?

Hell, last time was when she'd gotten divorced. She hadn't been in a serious relationship since. Therapy and Owen had helped her. They'd helped each other.

"Now tell us what the hell happened," Nina demanded.

Tess patted Nina's leg. "She'll talk when she's ready."

Digging into the pint of chocolate fudge ice cream, Evelyn waved a spoon. "You know most of it. Owen accused me of cheating on him with Donald. He said I always choose Donald over him. Which is bullshit, but I can concede that I did give Donald too much space in my life."

"And?" Nina prompted.

"I went to the firehouse and told Owen that he had a point. I had already thrown Donald out. I apologized for not thinking about how the decision to let Donald stay here would make him feel." She shrugged as if the next part was no big deal. "He said my apology didn't matter."

Nina shook her head. "Asshole. Gabe said he talked to him, thought he was coming around."

Evelyn laughed. "Oh, yeah, I'll be talking to Gabe. Did he tell you what he did?"

"Uh-oh," Tess said.

"He hacked security cameras and God knows what else to show Owen that I didn't cheat." She bit her trembling lip. "Owen called today and apologized. Then he let it slip that Gabe proved I wasn't lying."

Tess moved over and put her arm around Evelyn's shoulder. "Men can be really stupid."

A fresh round of tears filled her eyes.

"I'm gonna kill Gabe. I told him to stop being a dick. He just couldn't back off," Nina said.

Evelyn shook her head. "It wasn't cool for him to hack into my life, but he was being Gabe. In his head, that was going to fix it. In the long run, maybe it'll help Owen. Next time he's confronted with someone telling him the truth, he might not jump to the worst conclusions."

"Next time?" Nina asked.

"It won't be with me. He said he trusted me, and even when I apologized for neglecting his feelings, it wasn't enough. He still didn't believe me. Believe in us. I can't live like that."

"There's got to be something..."

Tess waved a hand. "If Evelyn doesn't think they're worth fighting for, that's her choice."

Why did that feel like an attack? "Would you?"

"I don't know. I know you love him. And he loves you. If he didn't, you sleeping with Donald wouldn't have knocked him on his ass. Trevor said he'd been by to see him and he's a mess."

"He created this mess."

"I'm not defending him. I'm speaking as someone who has misjudged. I didn't trust Miles when it came to my kids, and he proved me wrong. He screwed up along the way, but that's life. Learning to accept that has been hard for me."

"Do you think Owen can learn to accept that I'm going to have men in my life but that doesn't mean I'm going to sleep with them?"

"I don't know. What do you think?" It was such a typical mom move from Tess. She'd led Evelyn down a path to question her own thoughts and beliefs.

But this was such a mess. "I thought so. When we started this, moved our relationship to more than friendship, I thought we couldn't go wrong. We've always trusted each other. But he changed."

"You both did. Falling in love does that."

Nina watched the conversation like it was a tennis match. Evelyn tilted her head. "Anything to add?"

"I don't know. This whole thing is very disheartening for me. I thought you and Owen were a sure thing. I mean, if you guys can't make it work, how can the rest of us?"

"Hell if I know," Evelyn answered and scooped up more ice cream.

It had been days that felt like months since he had seen or talked to Evelyn. He'd fucked up everything, and he'd tried calling her, but she wouldn't answer. He attempted to get Nina or Tess to pass a message to her, but they weren't having any of it. At least Tess had given him a sympathetic look. Gabe had gotten him in trouble, and Trevor made it well known that he wasn't getting in the middle of anything.

So he did what he'd been dreading—he turned to his family. He called Dave and asked him to meet for early drinks. He sat at a corner table at the sports bar, completely uninterested in the game on TV, nursing a beer while waiting.

His brother slid into the chair across from him and said, "Tell me your troubles."

"I screwed up with Evelyn."

Dave waved a waitress over and ordered two more bottles of beer. "How bad?" he asked.

"Like take-the-few-things-from-my-house, return-my-key and pretend-I-don't-exist bad."

Dave let out a long, low whistle. "What the hell did you do?"

He drained his bottle and then launched into an explanation. Dave listened without interrupting.

When he finished, Dave sat back and crossed his

arms. "Let me get this straight. You accused her of cheating on you with her ex and in your apology, you pointed out that you were only apologizing because your buddy invaded her privacy to prove her honesty."

"It sounds even worse when you say it like that."

"Am I wrong?"

Owen shook his head.

Dave reached across the table and slapped the back of Owen's head. "What the hell were you thinking?"

"I don't know."

"I've watched you with Evelyn for years. I've never seen you as comfortable and in love as you are with her."

"I know." He held his head with both hands, elbows propped on the table. "Every time I saw her with other guys, just talking to them, it was like a switch flipped and I started looking for evidence. Then when I saw her ex in her house, I lost it."

"So instead of enjoying every minute of your life with the woman you love, you spent all your waking moments looking for proof that she was cheating. Not every woman is Stacy."

"I know that. But I missed all the signs with Stacy."

"You shouldn't have to look for signs. You made yourself see things that weren't there with Evelyn."

He knew this. With the exception of going to work, all he'd done was retrace every bad move he'd made with Evelyn. He even went back and talked to his old therapist. "I know my head is a mess. I need to figure out how to get her back."

Dave blew out a breath. "Evelyn is a strong-minded

woman. She's not going to put up with that kind of bullshit."

"Now you're an expert on Evelyn?"

"I've known her for years. I'm not an expert, but I know enough to know you delivered a hell of a blow, and you might not be able to come back from that."

"Then I guess this conversation is pointless."

"Have you seen her?"

He shook his head. "I've been trying to respect her privacy. She won't answer my calls or texts."

"She might respond to a face-to-face conversation. It would at least let you know where you stand. Look her in the eye and see if there's anything left."

His stomach turned thinking about how he'd treated her when she'd come to see him. Both times. He was such an asshole.

"But don't be creepy and stalkery about it, or I'll have to kick your ass. Don't lose sight of respecting her, but let her know you want to try to fix it. Show her you're willing to put in the work."

He looked at the time. Knowing Evelyn, she wouldn't be leaving work for a while yet. He passed his full beer to his brother. "I have an idea, but I have to go."

"What are you going to do?"

"I'm going to see her and ask her to go on a date."

"Good luck."

EVELYN HAD BEEN DOING LITTLE MORE THAN WORKING, but the extra time on the phone and behind the control panel was paying off. People were tuning in to *Chi-talk Live,* and the bonus for her was that she was too exhausted to think about Owen. She pulled into her parking lot, and her heart stuttered. The mere thought of Owen had her conjuring an image of his car. She hit the brakes and blinked.

His car was in her guest spot. She drove to her spot and when she angled, her headlights caught on Owen sitting on the ground. *What the hell?*

He looked up, squinted at the headlights, and used a hand to shield his eyes.

She rolled her window down, the cold fall air whipping in. "What are you doing?"

"I wanted to see you."

She waved a hand to get him to move. He stepped back to the wall and waited while she parked. She reached for her bag and took a few calming breaths. Owen was here. She had no idea why, but it felt so damn good to just see him. She reined in the swell of emotion and stepped from her car.

He must've been sitting there a while. His cheeks were pink from the cold wind.

"Why are you here?"

"I want to talk to you, if you'll listen."

"Sitting in my parking spot seemed like a good idea, why?"

"It got your attention, didn't it?" He offered a small smile.

A gust of wind kicked up and sent her hair flying.

"Can I come in? It's freaking cold out here."

"You have a key."

"After you returned my key, I thought you might've had the locks changed. Besides, it would be another douche move to just be sitting in your condo uninvited."

She heard his words. He was acknowledging that he'd crossed lines. It was a step in the right direction. She nodded and led the way inside.

Upstairs, she hung up her coat while he locked the door. Then she turned and crossed her arms while leaning against the couch.

He stood for a full minute and just stared into her eyes. The pain he was in radiated across the room, and she wondered if he felt hers as well. Then his gaze dipped, and she had her answer. He knew.

"I fucked up," he said quietly, not quite a whisper. He ran a hand through his hair and looked up again. "The thought of losing you made me unable to think straight." Raising a hand to stop the response from forming on her lips, he continued, "I know you did nothing to put those ideas in my head."

He paced in the small hallway. "I look at you and I see the most amazing woman I've ever met. I can't help but wonder what you're doing with me. Other men want you, and it fucks with my head. But I'm working on fixing that."

He stopped in front of her, close, but not touching. "I went to talk to my therapist. I'm trying to get it right, to show you that you can trust me not to screw this up again."

This was what she'd wanted before. An apology and the admission that he'd at least try not to constantly think she was cheating.

"I know I have to prove myself to you. All I'm asking for is a chance. Don't give up on me."

His plea ripped through her heart. Could they do this? She saw sincerity in his eyes. Her fingers flexed because she wanted so badly to touch him, soothe him. Find comfort together. But she simply whispered, "Okay."

Tess had made her question whether this relationship was worth fighting for. It was.

"Was that a yes?"

She nodded and leaned forward.

He gripped her hips and held her still. Leaning until his forehead touched hers, he said, "I love you so much. I've missed you."

Her heart thumped and her nerves sang. "I love you, too."

Then with his lips near hers, he asked, "Will you go out on a date with me?"

"Of course," she answered with a smile, still waiting for the kiss.

"I'd like you to be my plus-one."

Her heart swelled. He wanted them to be what they'd always been for each other before. Could they go back?

"It'll be a first date." He leaned around her and slid an envelope on the counter. "There's the invitation."

He kissed her cheek.

She turned her head to catch his mouth, but he stepped away. She sagged against the wall, her head spinning.

"I should go."

"Stay."

"I have to work in the morning."

"You can hang out for a while. We can talk and catch up."

They went to her couch and sat beside each other, touching in small ways. She told him all about the success of the show, and he thanked her for airing the segment about the youth center.

"I thought your boss shot that down," he said.

"He did, but in our first episode, we were still finding our rhythm. We had a guest who was horrible on camera, and we cut the interview short. I needed filler."

He huffed. "So I'm filler now, huh?"

"Never." She wrapped an arm around his torso and leaned on him. She inhaled his scent, which finally grounded her. Until this moment, she hadn't realized how off-kilter her life had been.

After they cuddled for a while, he kissed her head. "I really do need to go."

She got up and followed him to the door. On the way, she snagged the invitation he put on the counter. She opened the envelope and looked at it. The charity event Marilyn had organized for the youth center was Friday night.

"I have to wait two more days to be with you?"

After putting his jacket on, he turned and backed her into the wall again. "We're going to get this right this time." He pressed his entire body against hers.

His strength and heat enveloped her. She grabbed a fistful of his T-shirt as he lowered his mouth and kissed her. It was slow but needy. Her body buzzed and hummed with the desire crackling between them. When he pulled away, they were both breathless.

"I'm always thinking about you. Always," he murmured.

"I want to do more than think about you."

"Soon." Then he turned and left.

OWEN STILL HADN'T SLEPT WELL AFTER LEAVING EVELYN last night, but if he'd stayed, they would've had sex. Sex wasn't a problem for them. He needed to show her that he trusted her. He just wasn't sure how that was supposed to look. He'd finally realized that although she could have her pick of men, she'd chosen him. That's why they were each other's plus-one. No one was better.

He stretched out on his bunk to rest at the firehouse. His phone buzzed. A text from Evelyn.

Can we talk?

He hit send to call her. "What's up? You really couldn't wait until tomorrow to hear the sound of my voice?"

"The sound of your voice does some really amazing things for me, but this is a business call."

"When it comes to you, I only think of pleasure, not business."

She laughed. He hadn't realized how much he

missed that sound. Pushing up to sit, he asked, "What business?"

"Marilyn and I were talking about the benefit tomorrow night. Chi-talk Live has generated a lot of buzz. We were thinking it might be a good idea to bring cameras. Marcus, my boss, likes the idea. He thinks it'll be a boon for the show."

He waited, thinking there must be more.

"Owen?"

"Yeah."

"What do you think?"

"I'm not in charge of the center. And Marilyn has organized this entire thing with Sandra."

"But the center is important to you, and I don't want to encroach or exploit what you have going on. Not for my ratings."

How did they get here? "Babe, I know you wouldn't do anything to hurt the center or me. If you want to film the benefit, bring an army of cameras, as long as Sandra is okay with it."

"That means I'd be working on our date. I don't want you to feel like I'm ignoring you."

"Will you come home with me?"

"I would've done that last night."

"Then bring your cameras, and I'll watch you in action."

"There's one more thing." The way she spoke slowly, drawing out the words, didn't sound good.

"What?"

"We've had a lot of viewers ask about the hot firefighter. We want you on camera again."

He sighed. Being on TV wasn't something he'd ever

wanted. "I'd do almost anything for the center. Just don't ask me tough questions."

She laughed again. "I'm pretty sure you can handle yourself."

They disconnected so she could get back to work. Doing a segment from the benefit was going to add extra work for her, but she seemed happy to take it on.

Owen slid back down on the bed. Thinking about the success of her show and the benefit, he suddenly had an idea of how to show Evelyn he trusted her.

FOR THE NEXT DAY AND A HALF, EVELYN WAS RUNNING like crazy, but it was exhilarating. So much went into cameras going on-site. The equipment, the crew, release forms...she just hoped it would be worth it. After talking to Nina about Owen showing up at her place, Nina demanded she get a ticket to the benefit. She wanted to be there to witness the reunion or to rescue her if Owen messed up again.

Evelyn tried to reassure her that wasn't a possibility. He wasn't perfect, but he was getting his act together. She had faith in him. Nina arrived as Evelyn stood in front of her closet. She had nothing to wear to the benefit. She'd spent the last thirty hours or so planning the segment and she'd forgotten about planning for her date.

She opened the door for Nina. "I'm screwed. I have

nothing to wear. It's going to be the worst first date in history."

Nina laughed. "Not possible. I have the record for at least the top ten worst. There's no way that a new first date with a man you love, who also loves you, can be the worst. You can wear nasty sweatpants and he'd still want to do you."

Evelyn bit her lip. "Your classiness never fails to amaze me. Help me figure out what to wear. We have to leave soon."

Touching Evelyn on the shoulder, she said, "Move and let me do my magic."

Evelyn sat on the edge of her bed and watched as Nina slid hangers around for a minute before pulling some options out.

As she stepped into the first dress Nina picked, she tried to remember if she'd ever worn it with Owen. She wanted tonight to be special. Then her phone rang. Donald?

Waving at Nina as she tried to zip up the back of the dress, she answered, "Hello."

"I'm back in town lining up some prospects."

Of course he was. So typical for a man like him to be fine after one short news cycle. No one remembered the guy who did shoddy journalism. "Why are you calling me?"

"Because I received the strangest phone call yesterday. From Owen."

"Owen?"

Nina's eyes popped wide. She mouthed, "What?"

Evelyn turned away.

"He invited me to a benefit for the youth center. The

segment that you ran on the first episode, even though I was sure it was a bad move."

"I'm aware of the segment."

"He said that since I was an integral part of you getting Chi-talk up and running and since you'll be filming the benefit, I might want to be there."

Well, damn.

"What do you think?"

"I think you should keep lining up your prospects. Tonight isn't a place for you. Thank you for calling and asking, though."

"Anything for you, Ev—Evelyn. I want you to be happy."

"I am." She clicked off and turned to where Nina was bouncing on the bed.

"Well? Why is Donald calling you?"

"He was considering coming tonight." When Nina's face filled with concern, she added, "I told him not to."

"If I remember correctly, listening isn't his strong suit."

"It's okay. Let's go."

At the hotel where the benefit was being held, the crew was already setting up. Nina drove so that Evelyn could go home with Owen. As she talked to the crew, she kept an eye out for him. Marilyn was doing her thing and greeting guests and talking to hotel staff. The woman truly was amazing. As soon as Evelyn introduced Nina, Marilyn commandeered her friend. At least Nina wasn't watching her pathetically look for Owen.

Suddenly, a warm hand was on her back.

"Hello, beautiful."

She automatically turned into his arms and accepted

a kiss on the cheek. With a smile, she said, "We need to talk."

Taking his hand, she pulled him away from the room with the cameras. "Donald called me today."

"Yeah," he said cautiously.

"You invited him tonight?"

He nodded.

"Why the hell would you do that?"

He rubbed his thumb over her knuckles. "I'm not going to lie. I'm never going to like the man. But he is part of your life. He's part of the reason you have your job, which you love. How can I hate him if he was able to help you get what you want? Plus, I wanted you to see that I can be in the same room with him, while you look utterly stunning, and not hit him."

She laughed. "I don't even know where to start with that. Thank you for the compliment." She looked him up and down in his tux. "You're pretty sexy yourself."

Running a hand over his lapel, she considered how to address the rest. "Thank you for accepting my relationship with Donald. But he won't be coming tonight."

"Really? I thought for sure, he'd—" He stopped, probably realizing that whatever he planned to say next wouldn't sound too favorable.

"I told him not to come. Tonight is about us and the youth center you love. I would never want an extra person on a first date."

He kissed her softly. "You won't ever have to worry about that again, since this will be your last first date. Ever."

She wrapped her arms around his neck. "I like the sound of that."

OWEN WATCHED EVELYN BUZZ AROUND ALL NIGHT. HE'D talked to Marilyn in front of the cameras for a new segment, and then he'd spent time talking to other guests, trying to convince them to give more money than whatever outrageous amount Marilyn had made them pay for the privilege of being there.

He finally found Nina near the bar.

"It's about time," she said. "Are you ready?"

"Are you sure this is a good idea?"

"A grand gesture is always a good idea."

"Just make sure no cameras are on us. If she says no, I don't want that humiliation to be immortalized."

She smacked his arm. "Jeez. It's not like you're getting down on one knee and proposing." She paused. "Are you?"

"If I was going to do that, it wouldn't be here."

Nina nodded. "I'll go get her. Marilyn knows I'm going to call Evelyn out of here. In fact, she gave me the ammunition to pull her away." She gave him an evil little smile and walked away.

He patted the small box in his pocket. He'd considered popping the question, but it was too early, as silly as that seemed. They'd known each other for years. But this was a new start.

He briefly wondered what emergency Nina claimed, but he didn't stop to hear or watch. He moved to the small office Marilyn had set up for them to use. He paced the room, a little nervous. Not because he was unsure. He'd never been more sure of anything.

The door swung open, and Nina shoved Evelyn in.

"What?" she yelped, and then the door slammed behind her. She turned and saw him.

The look of shock gave way to love.

"What's going on?" she asked.

"I needed to see you. Ask you something."

"It couldn't wait?" She pointed at the door. "I have a crew out there."

"Marilyn has it handled. This couldn't wait." He stepped closer and pulled the small flat box from his pocket. "Nina said I needed a grand gesture to win you back. I personally thought biting back my attitude and calling Donald was a pretty big gesture, but she said I needed more. I needed to offer something that was the same size as the fuckup."

He took her hand. "The thing is, my fuckup was pretty big. So I'm just laying it out there." He put the box in her palm.

Eyeing him warily, she lifted the lid. She smiled at the picture of him and Probie.

"I love you, Evelyn. Probie and I want you back. All the time. Forever." He took the picture out so she could see the house key that she'd returned. "I don't want you to just have access to my house. I want it to be your house, too."

Her breath hitched.

"Move in with us."

She looked up at him with tears in her eyes. But she was still smiling. "Yes."

"You can take some time."

"Shut up and kiss me. I said yes." She launched herself at him, wrapping her arms around his neck and pressing her lips to his.

Kissing her was like coming home. He held her tight to him. When they paused to breathe, he asked, "How long till we can slip out of here?"

She gave him the smile that he knew was just for him. "Soon. But we don't have to hurry. We have forever, right?"

The only words that sounded better than "forever" on her lips came next. "I love you."

He had no doubts about their love or their future. He couldn't wait.

Also by Shannyn Schroeder

The O'Leary Family

More Than This (The O'Leary Family #1)

A Good Time (The O'Leary Family #2)

Something to Prove (The O'Leary Family #3)

Catch Your Breath (The O'Leary Family #4)

Just a Taste (The O'Leary Family #5)

Hold Me Close (The O'Leary Family #6)

The O'Malley Family

Under Your Skin (The O'Malley Family #1)

In Your Arms (The O'Malley Family #2)

Through Your Eyes (The O'Malley Family #3)

From Your Heart (The O'Malley Family #4)

The Doyle Family

In Too Deep (The Doyle Family #1)

In Fine Form (The Doyle Family #2)

Daring Divorcees Series

One Night with a Millionaire

My Best Friend's Ex

My Forever Plus-One

Stand Alones

Between Love and Loyalty

Meeting His Match

Hot & Nerdy

Her Best Shot

Her Perfect Game

Her Winning Formula

His Work of Art

His New Jam

His Dream Role

Sloane Steele's Books

The Counterfeit Capers

Origin of a Thief (The Counterfeit Capers 0)

It Takes a Thief (The Counterfeit Capers #1)

Between Two Thieves (The Counterfeit Capers #2)

To Catch a Thief (The Counterfeit Capers #3)

The Thief Before Christmas (The Counterfeit Capers #4)

Milton Keynes UK
Ingram Content Group UK Ltd.
UKHW021827260824
447290UK00008B/39